Under the Eagle's Wing

or
The Case of the French Embezzler

by G. H. Teed

Originally from the magazine,
Sexton Blake Library. No 21 New Series (2nd) 30 Nov, 1925.

A Tale of Sexton Blake, Tinker, and The Black Eagle.

Stillwoods Edition, 2019.

Stillwoods.Blogspot.Ca

Catalogue Information:
Title: Under the Eagle's Wing
Sub-Title: The Case of the French Embezzler
Author: G. H. Teed (1886-1938)
First Published: Sexton Blake Library, No 21 New Series (2nd)
30 Nov, 1925.
Illustrated by Arthur Jones
This Edition: Stillwoods, 2019
ISBN Canada: 978-1-988304-72-4
Blog: Stillwoods.Blogspot.Ca
Author's Blog: http://ghteed.blogspot.com/
Storefront: http://www.lulu.com/spotlight/lulubook22

Keywords: Sexton Blake, The Black Eagle.

A minor banking official becomes infatuated by Madame Goupolis, she of 'The Great Canal Plot'. She causes him to embezzle his bank as he favours her. After she has spirited away all she can get from him, she absconds back to safety in Egypt, leaving him to face up. But Andre Sartel kills two French Surete in his escape to London, seeking protection from none other than 'The Black Eagle'.

Sexton Blake is called in by the Surete—the case is international and urgent. Will Blake and Tinker be able to locate the offender before he can find safe ground?

G. H. Teed's books at Stillwoods Bookstore:

ISBN	Title
978-1-988304-69-4	The Secret of the Coconut Groves
978-1-988304-68-7	The Affair of the Six Ikons
978-1-988304-67-0	The Black Abbot
978-1-988304-66-3	The Crook of Marsden Manor
978-1-988304-65-6	The Tiger of Canton
978-1-988304-70-0	The Case of the Disguised Apache
978-1-988304-62-5	The Sacred Sphere
978-1-988304-60-1	Nelson Lee and the Lhassa Red Menace
978-1-988304-59-5	Bribery and Corruption
978-1-988304-57-1	Spies Ltd.
978-1-988304-56-4	Murder Ship
978-1-988304-55-7	Crooks' Vendetta
978-1-988304-54-0	Bottom of Suez
978-1-988304-53-3	The Mystery of the Kidnapped Killer
978-1-988304-52-6	The Clue of the Four Wigs
978-1-988304-51-9	Voodoo Island
978-1-988304-50-2	The Mystery of The Film City
978-1-988304-49-6	Hounded Down
978-1-988304-48-9	The Grey Ghost
978-1-988304-47-2	Five in Fear

http://www.lulu.com/spotlight/lulubook22

CHAPTER 1. Out of the Storm—Memories of Devil's Island—The Messenger from France.

THE BLACK EAGLE was back in London.

He was seated in the studio of the bizarre house he occupied —at times—in the quiet crescent off the Edgware Road, engrossed in touching-up some water-colour sketches he had made in Egypt, when his brother entered noiselessly and stood waiting just inside the door until the other should look up.

He stood there patiently, a queer, mis-shapen creature whose arms hung down like those of a great ape, whose back was humped in a twisted lump, whose squat legs were bowed almost to the width of a barrel and whose brow was low, as that of a primitive savage.

His strange yellow eyes, yellow with the yellow of amber, were fixed in dumb devotion on the stern, handsome profile of the man at the easel.

No observer would ever have guessed that these two were other—could be other than master and servant. And yet they were bone of the same bone, blood of the same blood, flesh of the same flesh.

The same mother had borne them, and there was between them a tie of affection which had held them together through every stress and twist of fate even though a long twenty years had passed, without either knowing whether his brother was living or dead.

Twenty years! Twenty years of sheer hell on Devil's Island for the one; twenty years of the worst type of hell-ships for the other.

The Black Eagle finished a little blotch of ultramarine sky which had been engaging his attention; then, laying down his brush, he turned, his whole face lighting up with a smile of affection as he did so.

"What is it, brother mine?" he asked.

No purer voice ever sounded from human throat than that which answered him. Low and clear it was, pure and resonant as the thrum of a silver bell.

"It is the buzzer in the hall, brother," was the response. "Someone is at the outer door."

The Black Eagle frowned, and reached for a cigarette.

"Someone at the outer door," he murmured. "That is strange, brother mine, for there is none, or should be none, to know that we are back in London."

He gazed upwards at the wide, semi-circular window above the wide gallery which ran all round the studio. The yellow silk curtains over it were drawn a little aside, and on the glass he could see the rain outside streaming down in a steady sheet.

"It still rains," he remarked, turning round to the hunchback. "Has the storm grown Jess?"

The other shook his head.

"It is worse," he answered. "It has grown to a gale, a wild gale."

"Um, and someone calls on such a night! Truly, his business must be of an urgent nature, and, since that is the case, brother mine, we shall have a look at our visitor before admitting him. He may not be alone."

With that, he rose and walked across to where the other stood. They passed out of the studio, into a wide' and lofty lounge-hall, which was furnished in the most sumptuous manner.

The furniture was almost entirely of Italian Renaissance, the rugs the very pick of the bazaars of Damascus and Baghdad, the pictures few in number, but each one a masterpiece, not the least among them being two which had been painted by the Black Eagle himself, or, as he was known in the world of art, David Stone.

He dropped the end of his cigarette into a big silver bowl which stood on a low table in the centre of the apartment; and was turning towards the short lobby which separated the inner door from the outer when the low buzzer sounded again. He made a sign to his brother, and strode to the right-hand wall of the lobby, inside, the hall. He stood close to this, and then, as he touched a switch, every light in the place went out.

He fumbled about for a second, and noiselessly opened a tiny panel, which permitted him to look out on to the porch without anyone there being aware that they were under surveillance. He saw the blur of a solitary figure pressing up against the door, as if to avoid the worst of the driving storm which was sweeping London. Then he softly slid the panel back into place, and turned on the lights.

"A solitary visitor," he said, in a low tone, to his brother. "Admit him."

He stood close to the centre table, a freshly lit cigarette between his fingers, while the hunchback shambled along through the lobby to the door, the only door which gave access to either front or side walls of the house.

A damp blast of wind swept in as he opened the portal, and the

Black Eagle could hear the mumble of voices. Then the door slammed, and the next moment his brother appeared, with an oddly garbed figure behind him.

The stranger was dressed in a long black rubber storm-coat and a short-peaked cap, which the Black Eagle recognised at once as the type of outfit peculiar to the fishermen of the Brittany coast in France.

He wore heavily-built, clumsy boots, and beneath his coat the Black Eagle could see the lower portion of coarse blue serge trousers.

The visitor removed his cap, and the Black Eagle studied the countenance which was revealed. It was the direct antithesis of the type which one would have expected to see beneath such a cap.

Instead of being rugged and seamed with the gales of many Brittany winters, it was round and soft-looking, podgy, and of that hue which spells only one thing—long dissipation.

He was clean-shaven, but the keen eyes of the other could make out the tell-tale patch on chin and upper lip which told him that not long since the man had worn both beard and moustache. His eyes were deep-sunk, tired. His whole attitude that of one utterly fatigued.

The Black Eagle made a gesture in the direction of his brother, and the latter drew off the visitor's rubber coat. Beneath, he was dressed in a blue woollen sweater and a blue reefer coat, and as the weight dropped from him, he came slowly across towards the welcome blaze of the big wood fire which was burning in the hearth.

The Black Eagle reached the hearth before him, and, turning, gave a slight bow.

"I was not expecting a visitor to-night, monsieur," he said slowly in French, all the while keeping his eyes fixed on those shifty ones, which tried again and again to hold his, but failed. "I cannot say whether you are welcome or unwelcome. Perhaps you will explain why you have honoured me by braving the storm."

The Frenchman thrust out his hands to the blaze, and rubbed them for a few moments before replying. Then, making, no attempt to disguise that his host had placed him quite correctly when he had addressed him in French, he said:

"You are he who is known as Monsieur David Stone?"

"That, monsieur, is correct."

"And by another name as well?"

"That, monsieur, may or may not be the case."

"I have come from a friend of yours, monsieur. I was given the address in London of Monsieur David Stone, and I was told that when I succeeded in finding him I would have found as well him whom I seek, and who is known sometimes as the Black Eagle."

"Ah!"

The Black Eagle uttered the exclamation quietly, quite in a conversational tone.

"Perhaps, monsieur, you will be good enough to tell me what friend this Monsieur David Stone possesses who takes such a liberty with his privacy."

"I shall do so, monsieur, but I must speak that name in private," and as he finished the stranger glanced towards the hunchback.

"What you have to say can be said before my brother," was the response. "And I shall be obliged if you will waste no more time, monsieur. I must know whether to offer you my hospitality or—something else."

The Frenchman stepped closer, and looked up at the harsh visage above him. He hesitated a second or so, then he whispered:

"Your name, monsieur—the name of Monsieur David Stone—was given to me by Madame Goupolis."

"Where?"

The voice of the Black Eagle was like the crack of a whip as he snapped out the question.

"In Paris, monsieur."

"Is this woman of whom you speak— Madame Goupolis, you said, did you not?— in Paris now?"

"No, monsieur. If she has been fortunate, she is safely in Egypt. But, believe me, monsieur, I speak the truth. She gave me another name to speak so that you would know that I did, in truth, come from her. Shall I speak that name?"

"Go on."

"Jules Vabour."

And then the Black Eagle knew that his visitor must indeed have seen Madame Goupolis, for none but the notorious, intriguing Greek woman knew what that name meant to the Black Eagle.

Jules Vabour! It was the name of a man who, when he had been on Devil's Island but two short years, had come out there as one of the higher officials of the terrible French penal settlement. It was the name of a man who had hounded the Black Eagle day and night, through some strange hatred, for nearly ten years before he was

4

recalled to France.

Jules Vabour! How vividly in his mind even now was that day when he knew that Vabour was leaving! How clearly he could see himself standing there in the sweating den of the inner prison yard, facing the man who had tried and tried again to break him, and had failed!

How clearly his ears still resounded with his own words as he swore, before half a hundred other convicts, that the day would come when he would leave Devil's Island, and that when he did he should search out Vabour and make him pay!

And Vabour had laughed!

Then, years later, when he had been paroled across in Cayenne, and from there had escaped across the border into British Guiana, where he had cleaned up a fortune in the diamond-mines of the little-known Essequibo, one of his chief cares was to start out on his search for Vabour.

But there had been other deeds to do first. He had had to seek out and take vengeance on those who had seen him falsely accused in Paris twenty years before, who had seen him go to Devil's Island for a crime he had never committed.

But Vabour's day had come, and it was through the international adventuress, Madame Goupolis, that he had at last got track of Jules Vabour.

On his return to France Vabour had entered the service of a big banking firm. Then he had fled after embezzling several million francs. Some woman had squeezed him as dry as a wrung sponge and then thrown him aside.

Madame Goupolis was that woman!

Easy was it then for her to betray Vabour into the hands of the Black Eagle. And she had done so—for a price; the price of a human life which the Black Eagle had paid. Then like the bird of prey after which his fellow convicts on Devil's Island had named him he had winged his way across the Mediterranean to Egypt and there carried out his vengeance. Once more he had stood face to face with Jules Vabour; but on the second occasion Jules Vabour had not laughed.

And now, through the raging storm which was sweeping across London this night in early autumn, a man came to his house to speak of Madame Goupolis and of Jules Vabour.

Who was this stranger whose face was the putty grey of the

dissipated boulevardier, but whose clothes were those of the rugged Brittany fisherman? Who was this flotsam of the storm who only recently had worn beard and moustache, where now his podgy face was clean shaven?

Who was this stranger, only too obviously disguised, who spoke of that woman of evil and of Jules Vabour?

The Black Eagle motioned him into a low chair. Then he looked across at his brother.

"Bring us a decanter and glasses, brother mine," he said evenly. "Our visitor is going to tell us what brings him to the nest of the Black Eagle."

CHAPTER 2.   A **Startling Story—The Claws of the Black Eagle—The Hunted Crook.**

THE Black Eagle poured a brandy and soda for his visitor and took a whisky for himself. The hunchback passed the tray and then betook himself to the upper regions of the house. The host raised his glass with a courteous inclination of the head and after taking a sip said:

"And now, monsieur, your name and your business."

The Frenchman drank a deep gulp of the spirit and set the glass down. He fumbled in his pocket and produced a little grey bag of caporal tobacco and a packet of "zigzag" papers.

He clumsily rolled a cigarette and thanked his host for the match which was held in readiness. Then, after casting a quick glance at the other, he leant forward until he was sitting on the very edge of the seat.

"I have told you, monsieur, how I found you," he said at length. "And I have told you the truth as I shall continue to tell you the truth.

"It was the condition on which Madame Goupolis told me where to find you. Moreover, I could not tell you anything else for I have come to seek your aid and protection."

"You travel too fast," returned the Black Eagle coldly. "Begin at the beginning, monsieur, I pray you. First—your name."

"My name is Andre Sartel."

"Andre Sartel! Methinks I have heard that name recently, monsieur. Am I correct?"

"It is likely if you have read the news from Paris."

"Which I have. And you are he?"

"Yes, monsieur."

"Proceed, please."

"If you have read the recent news from Paris you will know that I—that I am an embezzler, an absconder."

"The papers say to the tune of some ten millions of francs," murmured the Black Eagle.

"And for once the papers do not lie. That was the amount. You know the story of Jules Vabour. Can you not guess mine?"

The Black Eagle turned his head and regarded him. Then he laughed, long and almost soundlessly. At last he paused: "Mon dieu, monsieur! Am I to take it that you fell a victim to the—er, charms of the Goupolis?"

"Yes! That woman was my ruin!"

"Possibly. She has ruined many. And you can console yourself with the thought that you are but one in that army. I really must adjust my ideas of the lady. I did not think she would bring it off again. She seems to have booked you for a pretty sum, monsieur."

"Ten million francs, but I have still five million francs left. She did not get all."

"Let me have a few details, monsieur. I have read the papers, and I know that certain things—"

"There is little beyond the bare facts. Some months ago I met Madame Goupolis. Until we parted in Paris and she gave me your name I did not know she was so called. She came to Paris last spring and took a large 'hotel' in the Avenue du Bois. She spent money royally, and as her remittances came through the bank of which I was vice-director. I thought she must be very rich. Then she came to my bureau over certain details of a remittance, and I at once surrendered to her charms.

"I was invited to dine at her 'hotel.' From that on our friendship grew apace, and then—well, then, monsieur, she asked for an overdraft, and what could I do? Que voulez-vous? That was but the beginning. The overdrafts grew larger and larger until, to protect my own position, I was compelled to ask her to deposit securities to cover the amount. It was then nearly two million francs. She readily agreed to do so and brought me nearly five million francs in what purported to be Egyptian government bonds. I passed these to her credit, but, at her request, locked them in my own private safe. Against this I advanced her further sums, until she had had more than four million francs.

"That was three weeks ago. All this time I was in her company constantly. I was completely infatuated—utterly under her spell. Then we suffered very heavy losses through our branch in Saigon, in French Indo-China. That precipitated matters in Paris. I knew that a thorough overhauling of our securities must take place and I asked her if I could realise on her Egyptian bonds. And what do you think she did, monsieur?"

"I can guess," responded the Black Eagle dryly. "But go on, please."

"She laughed at me. Then, without the slightest hesitation, she told me that the Egyptian bonds were only forgeries. What could I do?

8

Figurez-vous. There was I responsible for her overdraft of nearly five million francs, and nothing but worthless paper to show for it. I was completely at her mercy. So I had to listen to her.

"She told me the only thing for us to do was to run for it. And if we were to do that it would be as well to take with us as much more money as possible. I had to agree, so we laid our plans. Everything was arranged that we should leave on a certain night. She said if we could reach Egypt she would guarantee that we should be safe. But on the very eve of our flight I found that she was playing me false.

"I found a letter which she had received and read it. That letter opened my eyes. I confronted her with it and again she only laughed. Then I was furious. I threatened her, but what could I do—I who was in fear every moment of arrest? So we came to terms. I gave her another million francs and we agreed to part. In return for this she gave me your name and address in London.

"That night we fled—in different directions. As I have heard nothing I assume that she got safely out of France. But I was not so lucky. I knew that all the ordinary ports would be watched. But I had a plan.

"For some years past I have had a summer place on the cliffs of Brittany where I have spent some months each season. I reached there in safety, and through the assistance of two trusted servants I made arrangements to be sent across the Channel to England. I was on the very point of starting—that was four nights ago—when I was surprised by two officials from the Paris Surete.

"There was no chance to elude them. I could not escape. There were only two things to do—surrender or light. I chose the latter course. I pretended that I was going to submit, but when I had them off guard I drew a pistol and shot. You say you have read the papers, so—"

"So know that you shot them both dead, monsieur," finished the Black Eagle calmly. "All the world knows that, monsieur. Proceed!"

"Through the good offices of my servants and some fishermen, I was put across the Channel, monsieur. A man with five million francs in his pocket can do much. I was landed on the south coast of the English county of Devon, I think it is called, and from there I have succeeded, by very slow and careful stages, in reaching here.

"So in that, at least, Madame Goupolis did not lie."

"And now that you are here, what is it you wish, monsieur?"

"What I have said—your aid and protection. For those I am willing to pay a high price, monsieur—any price you name up to half the amount which I possess."

"My aid—my protection! I do not quite understand. You must know, if you know anything, that I myself am fugitive from the police of France and England. What you have done in France does not concern me.

"Any man who kills among those dogs at the Surete, who strikes down those who sent me to twenty years of hell on Devil's Island, is doubly welcome. Until I die, my hand is against that country and all it means. But my aid—my protection—to use your own words, monsieur, que voulez-vous? What can I do? What will you?"

"I must find sanctuary, monsieur,"

"You will not find it in this country. The association between the police of London and Paris is too close."

"I am aware of that. It must be another country."

The Black Eagle smoked thoughtfully for some minutes. Finally:

"And what country is it that is in your mind to honour with your presence as a citizen, monsieur?"

Sartel flushed. The Black Eagle's tone was altogether too sardonic for his liking. But he was helpless to take exception to it."

"You thrust, monsieur," he protested feebly.

"I did not invite you here."

"But you—you, too, are fugitive from the police."

So far did Sartel get, and no further. As if he had been shot into the air by a steel spring, the Black Eagle came to his feet.

In the same motion the end of his cigarette was flung into the fire, and, before the startled Frenchman could even begin to grasp what was intended, the terrible hands of the Black Eagle were about his throat.

He lifted Sartel clean out of his chair. He held him off the floor, and, slowly and remorselessly, waggled his head from side to side.

"So," he snarled—"so it is thus that you speak, you rat! You will be a dead rat if such words ever pass your lips again! The Goupolis told you about the Black Eagle. Did she ever tell you how he killed his man? It was like this, you rat of the catacombs—like this! But just two snaps—one to the right, so, and one to the left, so. The Black Eagle never used the knife or the gun. His hands are sufficient, and the fraction of an inch more and your spinal column would have been snapped as clean as a clay-pipe stem. Faugh!"

With that he flung the terror-stricken man back into his chair, where he lay gasping, like a landed fish. His eyes were popping from his head; his lips were already swollen, and his tongue was striving to lick the empurpled flesh.

"I—I—I!—" he managed to slobber hoarsely, but the Black Eagle cut him short.

"Enough!" he snapped. "That is your warning—your only warning. Let even the breath of such words pass your lips again, and you die as one snuffs out a candle!"

He lighted a fresh cigarette and sat down. He took a drink of whisky, and then, as calmly as if he were calling a hand at cards, he went on:

"I asked you, monsieur, what country is it that is in your mind to honour with your presence as a citizen."

"I—do—not—know," the other managed to respond. "Turkey was safe, but no longer. There is Russia—China. I have friends on the China coast if I could reach there."

"Europe is out of the question," broke in the Black Eagle. "You might have had a sporting run for your money if you had not killed those two men from the Surete. But now every string will be tightened up. You should have gone with the Goupolis, and quarrelled after. In Egypt you would have been safe, with her as your friend. But as your enemy—" And he shrugged.

"But let me think," he went on. "All Europe, as I said, is barred. Even Germany is out of the question. The whole stretch from Oslo to Constantinople will be on the lookout for you. South Africa is the same. India and the British East are likewise out of the question."

"You might drop out of sight in America, but to do that you would have to pay a heavy price, and as soon as the crooks over there learned how much money you have, they would keep you hidden just as long as it lasted. Then they would throw you to the wolves, which, in your case, means the police.

"Canada is hopeless, as is every shred of British territory. South America is a possibility, also Central America—particularly Mexico. Russia would be all right if you could reach it from the Siberian side. You would never get past the police barrier on this side. And then, as you have said, there remains the China coast. Knowing what has happened, could you depend on your friends there?"

"Yes. Of that I am sure. I have done them big favours in the past."

"Gratitude and friendship to the influential director of a rich banking firm is one thing, to a fugitive embezzler and murderer is another. But if you feel sure of those friends, then it is, in my opinion, your best chance. But how to get you there—that is the question.

"You cannot travel through the Mediterranean and the Suez Canal. Every ship which passes that way will be searched for weeks—ay, months to come. Nor can you go by the Cape. You might get through to the Pacific by a sailing ship, if one can be found, but that might take a long time. And I can assure you, monsieur, that every day you remain London is just the same as an extra scrape of the razor on the back of your neck, to prepare it for the guillotine!"

The Frenchman shivered and closed his eyes. He sank back in his chair, and a sudden whimper shot from between his lips. The Black Eagle was not what one might call a pleasant sort of host. His words were too brutally direct for one who was fleeing from justice. But he continued as if he had noticed nothing.

"Lastly, there is the Panama Canal—or last but one," he said. "And that canal is as dangerous for you as the Suez. Which brings us to the only remaining route by which you have even the ghost of a chance of getting through."

"How do you mean, monsieur?"

"I mean across America—From New York to San Francisco, and thence across the Pacific to the China coast. And that, monsieur, will take a lot of money and time."

"But—but I will pay! I will pay well, monsieur. I have five millions of francs in good banknotes, which can be negotiated easily. Half of that will I give if you will help me."

The Black Eagle's lips curled.

"Five millions francs! Do you think five million francs, half of it or all of it, would influence me?" he asked harshly. "What is five million francs to me when I can lay my hands on ten times that sum—twenty times that sum—within twenty-four hours?

"It is not any sum of money you possess that will influence me to help you. It is something else—something far greater— something in which you have been but a poor instrument. But you have served. You have killed two of those whom I would wipe entirely from the face of the earth if it were in my power to do so. You have struck at the country which made of me a shameful thing for twenty years. You have put two notches in the stick of the long score which I keep. And for each and every notch on that stick I am willing to pay a high price—in gold or in any other way in my power. And for that reason, that reason alone, I will help you."

"Monsieur, monsieur, I thank you! From my heart—"

"Wait! What did you do after you landed on the English coast?"

"It was at a lonely part. I hid during the day-time and travelled on foot by night."

"Do you think you were regarded suspiciously?"

"I do not think so, monsieur. I found what water I needed in the rain-pools. I did not have to ask for food as I had sufficient with me. I spoke to no one, and I avoided the towns as I came along."

"You mean you covered the whole distance on foot?"

"Yes."

"Scotland Yard will be scouring the whole country for you. The Surete will have sent across a full description of you, and the police here are no fools. It is going to be most difficult to get you out of England, but I shall try.

"It will be no easier to get you into America, but there are more ways, in that problem, to consider. In any case, it will be necessary to spend money freely. If you wish my assistance on that understanding, I am ready to give it. But I promise nothing. If you are caught I shall leave you to your fate; and if you so much as breathe my name I shall find you out wherever you are and kill you by slow torture until you will pray for the mercy of the guillotine."

CHAPTER 3.   The Black Eagle's Guest?—A Visit to the East End of London—And a Trip to Rotterdam.

IT was considerably after midnight when the Black Eagle finished discussing matters with Sartel. When he had dragged from the Frenchman all the details he could regarding the affair which had begun with an infatuation for the Greek adventuress, and had wound up with the killing of two officers from the Surete, he gave him another brandy-and-soda, and then disposed of him curtly enough.

He touched the little silver bell on the table close to him. The tinkle brought the hunchback from upstairs, and to him the Black Eagle said:

"Monsieur will be our guest for a few days, brother. I leave him entirely in your charge. You will see that he is made comfortable, and receives what food he fancies. But on no account is he to stir from the room in which you instal him."

The hunchback made a gesture that he understood, and waited for Sartel to rise and follow him. The latter gulped down his drink and turned to his host.

"That sounds as if I were to be more your prisoner than your guest, monsieur."

The Black Eagle shrugged.

"Exactly!" he replied. "From now on, monsieur, until I release you, you may consider that your every movement will be dictated. The initiative will be mine; obedience will be yours. And now goodnight. Your affairs require considerable thought."

Sartel had the grace to take his dismissal without further grumbling. He rose and followed the hunchback up the stairs.

When they had disappeared from view the Black Eagle drew his chair closer to the fire and lit a cigar. He filled his glass with a final night-cap and then settled down to figure out how he could best plan to carry out the bargain he had made.

He had been perfectly sincere when he had told Sartel that his services could not be bought for money. He had not boasted when he said that he had made a large fortune in diamonds in British Guiana. It was simply a statement of fact, and his fortune was now safely invested in the very safest form of Government securities.

Although his own personal wants were simple enough, he spent very large sums in the course of a year, for his movements were usually of the sort that called for a big income to cover them, and in order to carry out any scheme of vengeance or criminal coup on which he was engaged he would spend money like water to attain his ends.

But even at that and, with the extremely generous allowance he made his brother, he could not get through more than half of his income except by paying an enormous price for some old master or antique bit of furniture which struck his fancy.

Therefore, it was for no part of the five million francs that he had agreed to help Sartel. In fact, if Sartel had been of any other nationality, the Black Eagle would have kicked him into the road to fend for himself.

He held the Frenchman in utter contempt, for he had no patience with the man who would make a fool of himself over a woman.

The Greek woman, Madame Goupolis, had once tried to penetrate the armour of his cold reserve in Monte Carlo, but her arrows had glanced off without even leaving a scratch.

The Black Eagle knew women as he knew men, and it was his opinion that nine hundred and ninety-nine out of every thousand were out for just one thing—self.

But, like Jules Vabour before him, Sartel had succumbed, apparently without the slightest attempt at a struggle. And the Black Eagle could understand easily enough how the game had been played. But that type of crime left him cold.

Only a weak fool could plunge into such certain disaster, and only an addle-pated idiot could get so rattled as to clinch his every chance by killing two police officers. Much better it had been for him to hide what he had left of the loot and then give himself up.

The excuse of a "liason" in the French courts is looked upon as a strong reason for the backsliding of men, and Sartel, on that plea and with what political influence he might summon to his aid, might have got off with a comparatively light sentence.

But to kill two officials of the Surete! That was a very different matter.

Since the war a much closer accord had existed between Scotland Yard and the Paris Surete. In Paris there was constantly on duty, as the Black Eagle knew, a liason officer from Scotland Yard, and at the Yard a French liason officer from the Surete.

Therefore he knew it was dead certain that at the moment, the Yard was in possession of full particulars of the killing of the two

Surete men in Brittany. That meant that the net was already out.

It meant that every possible port of entry and embarkation would be under the closest surveillance. Air ports, too, would be combed, and if a man was to slip through he would need to display no little ingenuity.

Sartel had come in safely. The fool had hit on the only means by which he could have done so. But to get out—that was another matter. But it had to be done, some way.

The Black Eagle pondered the problem for hours before he finally rose and turned out the lights.

But he was abroad early in the morning despite the fact that he had had less than four hours' sleep, and, after a light breakfast, he called his brother into the studio.

"Have you seen our guest this morning, brother?" he asked.

"Yes, brother mine. He did not sleep well, but has had some food. I have put him in the room at the back with no windows except in the roof. I have also taken away his clothes and given him others to wear while he is here. He had a wallet which I allowed him to keep. He asks if he can speak with you."

"No. I have nothing to say to him—yet. Watch him carefully, brother. If he takes it into his head to go abroad he will get us all into trouble. I have told him I will help him, and I will, but only on my own terms. I am going away."

The yellow eyes of the hunchback clouded.

"Not for long, brother?" he asked anxiously.

"I do not know. I do not think so. I hope to be back within a few days. I am going abroad—to Holland. But our guest is not to know that. Then I have much to do here in London if my visit to Rotterdam is a success."

"Fear not, brother, he shall know nothing. And everything will be quite safe until your return."

The Black Eagle smiled affectionately.

"Well, I do know that, Paul," he answered. "You are as myself."

He had his answer in the flash of devotion which came into his brother's eyes, but the hunchback did not speak.

The Black Eagle left the house shortly after ten o'clock. Unlike Sartel, he made no attempt to disguise himself. As a matter of fact, although he had spoken only the truth when he had said that he, too, was a fugitive from the police, he was not much in fear of being molested.

Scotland Yard knew of his existence, but they possessed no records, either photographic or otherwise, by which to identify him.

The only person in London whom he had really to fear on that score was the private criminologist, Sexton Blake, of Baker Street, and he figured he could keep away from that individual's vicinity.

He took with him a small suitcase, and after taking a taxi to his bank, drove to Liverpool Street, where he booked a seat in the Pullman car on the eight-thirty boat express train leaving that night for Harwich and the Hook of Holland. He checked his bag in the cloak-room, and then walked along to the Great Eastern Hotel grill-room for lunch.

It was getting on for two o'clock when he emerged from the hotel and signalled to a taxi. He gave the man an address in Aldgate, and there he got out in front of the Three Nuns' Hotel—the great East End resort of seafaring men and those connected with the shipping industry.

He dismissed his taxi, and, entering the hotel, made his way to the bar. From there he could, by taking up his stand near the end door, survey almost the whole of the grill-room.

He sipped his drink leisurely the while he watched the various men who were still at lunch, and then, as he saw two individuals rise and come towards the bar, he moved away and took up his position where they must pass close to him.

As he had anticipated, they entered the bar and called for liqueurs. One was a thick-set, middle-aged man in what even a landlubber could have told were the shore-going clothes of a seafaring man. The other was a little Jew so common along Aldgate and the Commercial Road.

Neither of them had noticed the Black Eagle, for he had kept his back turned, but when they finished the drink and turned to leave, the Black Eagle shifted along quickly and laid one hand on the Jew's arm. The latter turned like a flash, for a touch on the arm is not popular in the East End.

As his eyes encountered those of the Black Eagle a quick surprise filled them and his jaw dropped. But before he could speak, the Black Eagle made a gesture enjoining silence. He put out his hand, which the Jew shook limply.

"I want to see you on business," said the Black Eagle in an

ordinary tone. "Can you arrange an appointment for this afternoon? I am leaving London to-night."

And because he knew the mild request was a command which he dare not disobey, the Jew nodded.

"I can see you here or at my office," he answered.

"Make it your office. What time will you be free?"

"I am just finishing cleaning up the details of a charter party with this gentleman here," was the response, as the Jew indicated his companion. "We are, nearly, finished. How will half-past three suit you?"

"First rate! I shan't keep you long. It is only a small booking of cargo I wish to arrange."

The Jew moved off then, and the Black Eagle stuck in the bar until closing-time. Then, with one of his own cigars between his teeth, he walked along the Commercial Road until he came to a very dingy building, outside of which there was a tarnished brass plate announcing that inside were the offices of "Abe Manstein, Shipbroker and Steamship Agent."

The Black Eagle passed through the doorway and up a rickety flight of steps to the first-floor. There were two doors there, each fitted with a dirty ground-glass, panel. On one was the single word "Private," and it was there the visitor knocked.

A voice bade him come in, and he pushed the door open to find the Jew seated at a roll-top desk dictating to a young woman. As he saw the Black Eagle, the Jew dismissed the girl, and when the door of the adjoining room had closed after her, the visitor slumped into a chair.

"Well," he inquired casually, "how is business?"

The Jew shrugged.

"Rotten!" he said succinctly. "I did not know you were in London, Mr. Stone. Have you some business for me? I hope so."

"I may have. I am going across to Rotterdam to-night. I expect to return in a few days. Before I go I want some information, if you can give it to me."

"You have but to command me, Mr. Stone. I have not forgotten our last deal. You treated me like a gentleman, and I shall be only too pleased to do further business with you."

"You ought to have been satisfied, considering that it put two thousand pounds cash into your pocket," remarked the Black Eagle.

"But there is more in this new affair than that—if you can handle it. I can't tell just what plans I shall lay until I have been to Rotterdam. Now, what I want from you is this—I want a letter of introduction to someone of your own trade and profession in Rotterdam; someone I can trust absolutely. I shall pay well."

The Jew smiled and shrugged.

"That is too easy, Mr. Stone. I can give you a letter to my own brother. Moses."

"Ah! I wasn't aware you had a brother there. Is he a shipbroker?"

"He is that—among many things."

"Good. You know as well as I do that a good many cargoes of whisky and wines are being run through to America with Rotterdam as a starting-point."

"Of course; it is no secret,"

"Will your brother have the entre to that crowd?"

"If he hasn't, then I don't know Moses, and he is no brother of mine."

"Well, give me a letter to him. Make it quite plain that I am to be trusted. I can put him in the way of a nice little bit of business."

"And me—do I get a bit of commish, Mr. Stone?"

"You get a thick ear if you haggle over that letter," responded the Black Eagle grimly. "Your turn will come when I return."

The Jew took no offence. He drew a private writing-pad towards him and at once set to work to write a letter of introduction to his brother. When he had finished he gave it to the Black Eagle to read, and the latter expressed himself as quite satisfied with the contents. As he watched Manstein fold it and put it in an envelope, he said:

"That will do as it stands. See that you don't send another one of a different nature by post, or a telegram cancelling anything you have said in this."

The Jew threw up his hands.

"Me, Mr. Stone?" he cried. "Me? I hope I may die if I would do such a thing to a nice gentleman like you!"

"That's enough. Give me the letter and I'll be off. I expect to be back in something under three days. I'll come on as soon as possible to see you. Three days— that will be on Thursday. If I reach Harwich that morning, look for me Thursday afternoon at this time."

With the letter of introduction in his pocket, the Black Eagle descended to the street. He had completed his business in the East

End sooner than he had expected, and, since his train did not leave until eight-thirty that evening, he had still something like four hours to put in. But that did not worry him.

Instead of returning west, he walked briskly along the Commercial Road until he saw a taxi coming along. He hailed this and told the man to drive along West Ferry Road to the Millwall Docks.

He got out there, keeping the man waiting, and for the better part of an hour he idled about the docks, apparently only casually interested in the various craft and their places of registry.

From there he drove to the East India Docks, but, although there were more and larger ships to be seen there, he did not stay long. He re-entered the taxi and ordered the man to go to Liverpool Street, and there he descended in front of the Great Eastern Hotel.

He had tea in the lounge, where he spent some time over the evening papers. He found considerable space in two of them devoted to the latest Paris scandal, and he was interested to read that, owing to the heavy defalcations of one of the senior directors of the bank in question, it was rumoured that it would be unable to meet its engagements.

But what held his attention most was the theory advanced by the Paris police as to the probable movements of the fugitive after he had killed the two officers in Brittany.

It seemed that they had not yet definitely established that any of the numerous fishing craft along the coast had put across to England, but there were three boats reported as being delayed out in the Channel.

In view of the gale which had been raging for two days it was thought generally that they had been blown well down Channel and had had to run before the storm.

But the police did not make any secret of their suspicions that the fugitive had been on one of those boats, and that he was trying to reach Ireland.

England, too, was mentioned, but it seemed to be thought that he would have little chance of landing in the latter country without being discovered. At which the Black Eagle smiled.

He made his way into the station about a quarter to eight and boarded his tram. He sat reading there until the train pulled out, and then he had dinner. They reached Harwich a few minutes past ten, and he went straight on board the steamer for the Hook.

It was a rough crossing, but that did not disturb the Black Eagle. He sat in the saloon for some time, eating a light supper and disposing of a couple of whiskies; then he turned in and did not come on deck until his steward called him at half-past five the next morning, to tell him that they would be at the Hook in half an hour.

He dressed leisurely, sipping his early morning coffee as he did so, and when they docked he was all ready to descend. He went straight to the train for Rotterdam, arriving there a few minutes before seven o'clock.

He had been in the Dutch city before, so drove to the hotel where he had stayed on previous occasions. He secured a room there, had a bath, changed and then breakfasted.

He sent out for the morning papers, but found nothing new about the Paris affair. He sat in the hotel lounge for some time smoking, but as the hands of the clock showed half past nine, he rose and made for the entrance.

He secured a cab and drove in the direction of the waterfront, having given the driver the address which Abe Manstein had written on the letter of introduction.

The cab drew up before a building which was outwardly and inwardly almost as dirty in appearance as the one in the Commercial Road, where Abe Manstein conducted his very intricate and, more often than not, shady business.

The Black Eagle dismissed the cab, and on the second floor found the office of Moses Manstein.

There were three rooms in all, but the Black Eagle knocked sharply on the one which was marked "Private" in Dutch. He did not wait for a summons to enter, but turned the handle and pushed the door open.

He paused on the threshold in sheer amazement for, at first glance, he could almost have sworn it was Abe Manstein himself who sat at the roll-top desk. Then he stepped inside and closed the door.

"Are you Mr. Morris Manstein?" he asked curtly in English.

The little Jew at the desk nodded.

"That iss my name," he responded, with a much more pronounced accent than his brother possessed. "Vat iss it I can do for you, zur?"

"I have a letter of introduction from your brother, Abe Manstein, of the Commercial Road, London. Will you receive it."

He held out the envelope as he spoke, and the Jew took it. He did not open it at once, however, but rose and effusively dusted a chair for his visitor.

"Tou vill be Mr. Shtone, no?" he said. "My bruzzer, Abey, he bass sent me one telegram about you. I haf been eggspegding you, Mr. Shtone."

The Black Eagle smiled slightly and sat down. He courteously refused the Jew's offer of a cigar and lit a cigarette. He had once been careless enough to accept a weed from Abe.

"I shall be obliged if you will be good enough to read his letter," was all the Black Eagle said.

The Jew sat down and broke the envelope which the bearer had sealed. He read the contents and looked up.

"It iss joost about what Abey hinted in hiss telegram," he said. "And now, Mr. Shtone, what iss it I can do for you."

"Abe tells me that you do some in the shipbroking line."

"That iss so."

"I take it, then, that you know something about the liquor shipments which leave this port for America."

Moses laid one finger along the side of his prominent nose; then he winked.

"If it wass anyone, else, Mr, Shtone, I woult say I know noddings. But after Abey's letter I say 'yess.'"

"Do a little in that line yourself, I imagine."

"Perhaps yess and perhaps no. I must know what it iss you wish, zur."

The Black Eagle tossed away the end of his cigarette. He was getting tired of fencing.

"I will tell you," he said curtly. "I want to get in touch with someone who is running a cargo of liquor through to New York."

"It iss then that you haf somedings to ship too?"

"If you mean liquor, then—no. I am not in that game. If you answer my question I will tell you just what it is."

"I say zen, Mr. Shtone, that I can put you in touch wiz a very goot man."

"Is he sailing soon?"

The Jew thought for a few minutes; then:

"One I know he iss sailing in two days. Anozzer, a very goot man, will be sailing in about one week."

"The latter interests me most, for I must return to London. Now look here, my friend, I will tell you what I want, I am willing to pay well for the service, and your brother in London will tell you that I am perfectly safe to deal with."

"I know zat, and I am content, Mr. Shtone. Vait vun moment, I beg you." With that the Jew rose and, opening the door leading to the next room, spoke to the typist in Hebrew. When he returned to his desk he remarked:

"Now ve shall nott be dissturbed, Mr. Shtone. I lissten vith all mine ears."

Then the Black Eagle began to speak slowly and in low tones. The Jew kept his word about listening, for he bent forward and did not miss a single syllable. Nor did he make any comment other than to nod his head from time to time.

When the Black Eagle finally paused, Manstein smiled.

"Vhat you vish it is not easy, Mr. Shtone. But it can be done—for a price. How much vould you be villing to pay?"

"Five hundred pounds to you, and the same amount to the captain of the ship."

The Jew made a pencilled calculation, changing that sum into guilders; then he nodded:

"If I did not vish for udder bissness in zo future vith you, Mr. Shtone, I vould ask for more. But no. I vill be eassy to deal vith. For me, I aggsept. For ze captain, I say yes, but I must see him to be sure."

"That is quite all right. How long will it take you?"

"If he iss in Rotterdam, zen I can see him to-day. If he is at his home in Amsterdam it will take more time. If he iss there I shall send him a telegram and he vill come to me."

"I am anxious to get back to London inside three days. Your brother is handling matters over there for me."

"I can bromise you not more zan two days, Mr. Shtone."

"Very well. I shall be at the X—Hotel; room number seventy-nine. You can get in touch with me there as soon as you know. And, remember, I want quick action."

CHAPTER 4.   All Arrangements Made for Sartel's Escape—A Big Surprise, and a Fool's Trick.

MOSES MANSTEIN was as good as his word. It was just four o'clock on the second afternoon when the Black Eagle, who was idling in the lounge of the hotel wondering if, after all, the Jew would fail him, was called to the telephone. At the other end of the wire he recognised Manstein's voice.

"Can you gome to my office, Mr. Shtone?" he heard.

"At once?" he asked,

"Yess—now."

"Very well, I shall come on immediately."

He hung up and got his hat and coat. Then he summoned a cab and told the man to drive to the water-front. On reaching Manstein's office he found, in the private room, a thin, snaky-looking individual, who was presented to him as Captain Gemeaker. He shook hands with this person who appeared to be most gloomy and morose of manner. Then Manstein got down to brass tacks without any preamble.

"I haf told what it iss you vant to Captan Gemeaker," he said. "He iss reaty to aggsept, but he vants an extra huntret pounts for hiss grew."

The Black Eagle turned to Gemeaker.

"Do you speak English?" he asked curtly.

"As you might say," was the answer in the strongest of American accents. "I have been sailing into New York for twenty years. I get you, Mr. Stone. I know what you want, but it ain't too easy, believe me. But I'll do it. I've got a smaller cargo than usual this time, and it don't pay so hefty as some people think—what with hanging off and on along the twelve mile limit and peddling the stuff over the side.

"Then there's the 'highjackers' to figure on. They are getting worse every trip, and we have to carry a special guard to deal with them. So any little extra is welcome. But as I've been tellin' Mose I must have somethin' to slip the crew. An extra hundred pounds would do the trick. I want a clean five hundred for myself."

"And for that you will carry out the whole job?"

"I sure will. Mose tells me you are a man of your word. Well, he'll tell the same thing about me. Shake hands on the deal, and you can bet your bottom dollar I won't let you down."

The Black Eagle shot out his hand, and the next moment the captain came out of his chair with a yell of pain, almost choking a quid of tobacco as he did so.

He little knew that he had been gripped by what no less an authority than Sexton Blake had said was probably the most powerful hand possessed by any living man.

But then, unlike Blake, he had not seen that pair of hands tear three packs of cards in half as easily as the average man would rip a visiting card in two. And while he had gone through the hard apprenticeship of the real sea, an apprenticeship in sail— he had not given nigh on twenty years to the purposeful development of certain sets of muscles.

The Black Eagle released his hand and allowed him to sink back. The seaman nursed his injured paw and tried to speak but couldn't, and contented himself by glaring.

"It is a bargain, then," announced the Black Eagle coolly. "What day do you clear, captain?"

"S-S-Sunday night," stammered the other.

"Sunday night. Can you wireless me on Saturday, or rather wireless Mr. Manstein's brother, the exact hour?"

"Yes, sir!"

The Black Eagle did not even smile at that concession.

"Very well. And in that message will you put the exact position you should be at midnight Sunday?"

"Yes, sir!"

"Then we can conclude our business, and I shall be able to get back to London tonight."

As he spoke, the Black Eagle drew out a thick leather wallet, and, opening it, abstracted a thick wad of banknotes. He counted off two hundred and fifty pounds which he handed to Moses Manstein.

"Two hundred and fifty pounds down now, Mr. Manstein," he remarked pleasantly. "I shall pay the balance to your brother, Abe, and ask him to remit it to you. No receipt will be necessary."

As he spoke the last words the Black Eagle's hard eyes held those of the Jew for a few moments, and in that brief space of time Moses Manstein determined that never, at any time, and on no consideration would he ever play this man false. He had a funny creepy feeling along his spine at the very thought of doing so.

"And you, captain," continued the Black Eagle, "I shall also pay you two hundred and fifty pounds now. The balance, as well as the hundred for your crew, I shall place in your hand as soon as my leg is over the side of your ship. Is that satisfactory?"

"Perfectly, sir. What you say goes with me,"

Then the Black Eagle rose. He shook hands again with them both, even though the pair looked as if they would gladly have dispensed with the formality; then he turned.

"On Saturday, then, captain, I shall look for your advice. That is understood?"

"Perfectly, sir."

And then he was gone.

The Black Eagle caught the evening train for the Hook of Holland. He boarded the Harwich boat there, and secured a cabin. He had dined at his hotel in Rotterdam before leaving so he went straight to his cabin.

He noted with satisfaction that the sea was considerably smoother, and the glass rising. The higher the barometer the better for his plans.

They docked at Parkeston Pier just about seven the following morning. The Black Eagle was one of the first ashore and almost the first in the breakfast car. In fact, so briskly did he move, and so little attention did he pay to anyone else that he entirely missed seeing a couple pacing up and down the platform waiting for the train to pull out.

If he had only looked their way he would have felt a little perturbed that he had been seen to land from the Dutch boat, for it was one of Black Eagle's tenets that no professional criminal should ever leave a single thread end sticking out.

It was Sexton Blake, the famous detective and his assistant, Tinker, whom the Black Eagle had failed to see.

But Blake had seen the Black Eagle, and as he disappeared into the breakfast car Blake caught his young assistant by the arm and hurried him along towards a coach at the rear of the train.

"Hard luck, my lad," he said, as he bundled him into an empty first-class compartment. "We shall have to wait until we reach London before taking breakfast."

"Why, guv'nor?" mumbled Tinker, in a disgruntled tone. "Gee! I'm as hungry as a hunter."

Sexton Blake smiled.

"I know, young Un. So am I. But we shall have to wait. There is an old acquaintance of ours in the breakfast car and I do not wish him to see us."

"Who is it, sir?"

Blake bent over and whispered a name in the lad's ear.

"Him!" exclaimed Tinker in amazement. "He's got a nerve, guv'nor, coming back to England after that last business in Egypt."

(Tinker was referring to the great affair of the Suez Canal when the Black Eagle had been mixed up in Prince Menes' plot to blow up the canal as a first crack at England. In that plot were also, Madame Goupolis, Prince Wu Ling, George Marsden Plummer, Mathew Cardolak, the mystery millionaire, and his henchmen the Three Musketeers. A record of the case appeared in the Sexton Blake Library under the "case index" title: "The Great Canal Plot." Ed.)1

"Nerve or not, it is he," rejoined Blake. "We'll stick in here and keep an eye on him after we reach Liverpool Street."

So Tinker, despite his hunger, was obliged to bow to Blake's dictum. But he was not gloomy for long; he was too used to the sudden shutting off of meal hours to worry for more than a passing moment. All the same he wished he had ordered something at the Alexandra Hotel in Dovereourt Bay before they had driven down to the train.

He and Blake had come down to Harwich the previous day on the trail of a diamond thief who had got away from Hatton Garden with a nice little bunch of uncut stones.

The fugitive had been on the very point of boarding the boat for the Hook of Holland the previous evening when Sexton Blake had touched him lightly on the shoulder.

That had finished the business, and at that moment, as the boat train pulled out for Liverpool Street, the diamond thief was safely behind the bars of Harwich gaol while the packet of uncut stones was locked up in Sexton Blake's travelling bag.

At Liverpool Street Blake took a taxi straight to Hatton Garden in order to pick up his client and take him on to Scotland Yard. They had kept well out of the way at the station until they had seen the Black Eagle pass between the iron gates.

Then Blake had sent Tinker after him with instructions to track him until he went to earth.

As for the Black Eagle he was quite unaware of the nearness of

---

1 Also - with a slightly different cast, **Bottom of Suez,** a Stillwoods publication.

his old enemy. Blake was the one person in London who would have recognised him at a casual glance, and he was, too, the last person the Black Eagle would have chosen to run up against.

But never a suspicion that he was being trailed crossed his mind as he entered a taxi and drove to his house in the quiet crescent off the Edgware Road.

And with that Tinker was content. He knew it was there the Black Eagle sometimes hung out when in London, and he figured that he intended making it his headquarters on this occasion for a time at least.

His chief aim just then was to get back to Baker Street and raid Mrs. Bardell's larder, and he had no idea that the Black Eagle was returning after only a three days absence.

When he had changed the Black Eagle got through on the telephone to Abe Manstein. He was guarded in what he said, and informed the Jew that he would call on him that afternoon at three o'clock.

Then he went up to visit his "guest." His brother had already reported that while Sartel had been restless he had not given any particular trouble. But on the Black Eagle's entrance the Frenchman jumped up. eagerly.

"You are back!" he cried. "Mon Dieu, monsieur, I thought you would never come. I have had the papers each day. The English police are searching every place for me. It will be impossible for me to get out of this country."

"Not so fast, monsieur," responded the Black Eagle. "I have been engaged on your affairs, and I have everything arranged. We shall leave here on Saturday night."

"But how—how will we escape the police?"

"That is my affair. It is yours to obey as I have already charged you. And now for what I have come to speak about. You have your money with you?"

"Oui, monsieur!"

"Let me have it."

"All, monsieur?"

"Certainly. Was that not a bargain?"

"You fool! Must I take you again by the throat? Do you think I want your filthy money for myself? Do you think you can travel abroad with nothing but French notes of a high denomination? They

28

must be changed, and you will lose something on the transaction, for there is a risk. But I shall arrange that. Give me the money."

The Frenchman obeyed, for, in truth, he could do nothing else. The Black Eagle slipped the wallet into an inner pocket without opening it; then, before leaving, he said:

"Remember, we leave here Saturday and one false move on your part means disaster."

He remained in his studio until his brother came to tell him lunch was ready.

Early in the afternoon he telephoned to a certain small garage, with which he had a secret agreement, and in a few minutes a big black car was at the door.

He drove through in this to the Commercial Road, and, at precisely three o'clock, walked into Abe Manstein's private room.

He remained with the Jew for the better part of an hour, and before he left, Manstein had promised that what he wished done should be accomplished.

"I took the hint you gave me before you went to Rotterdam," he said. "I have spent a good deal of time looking about, and I have found the man you want. He is ready. He wanted to sail to-morrow, but I can persuade him to put it off until whatever hour you wish on Saturday."

"That hour will be the one mentioned in the wireless message you will receive that day. Get on the 'phone to me the moment it comes and let me know just where this man thinks it will be best to pick us up. He has agreed to the price— five hundred!"

"He will be satisfied with that. And me, Mr. Stone?"

"There is something else for you to do. I am going to pay you two thousand pounds for what you do in this business which we have already discussed. And there is another two thousand for you if you can carry out another commission for me."

The Jew's eyes glistened at the mention of the sum. He was thinking that this mysterious man was well worth working for.

No one else had ever proved quite so lucrative an employer to Abe Manstein, and Abe Manstein's god was, first, last, and all the time, money.

"I will do my best, sir." he answered. The Black Eagle pulled out the wallet he had forced Sartel to give him. He opened it and took out wad after wad of banknotes. The Jew gasped in amazement at the sum, but the Black Eagle might have been handling so much waste paper for all it seemed to matter to him.

"I have counted this," he remarked, as he tossed the last bundle carelessly on the desk. "You will find exactly four million, five hundred thousand francs. I have retained, the balance. Those notes are quite genuine and cannot be traced as you know. But for certain reasons I do not wish to change them. That is a job for you. At to-day's rate of exchange that bundle is worth approximately fifty thousand pounds. That is taking a round rate of the day.

"But if you threw that amount of francs on to the market all at once sterling would jump several points, so I am going to allow for that. What I want from you is forty-five thousand pounds in sterling. That leaves you a margin of five thousand pounds to work on. You ought to be able to clean up three or four thousand, but certainly not less than two thousand.

"I want it done before Saturday morning. You need not give me a receipt. I realise it is a very large sum to pass over in this informal way, and it would tempt a good many men to clear out. But you will not do that. If you should be tempted to think about such a thing just remember that inside twenty-four hours I should find you and break your neck just as I would kill a chicken. Do you understand?"

"Yes. Mr. Stone, yes, indeed," stuttered Abe. "I should never think of such a thing, sir. You can trust me. I shall do my best."

"I am sure you will," responded the Black Eagle as he rose.

And thus things remained until early Saturday afternoon when Manstein telephoned him to tell him he had received a message from Captain Gemeaker. He read it over the wire and then in cautious tones began to tell the Black Eagle what plans had been made for that night. But the Black Eagle cut him short.

"Have you got that money?" he asked curtly.

"Yes, sir, every penny. It was not easy, but I managed it."

"Good. Wait at your office. I am coming on at once."

He then rang off and less than an hour later was once more sitting in the Jew's private room. Their business did not take long on this occasion, and as soon as they had completed it the Black Eagle drove back to the crescent.

Before dismissing the car he had a conversation with the driver, and then, once inside the house, he went upstairs to see Sartel. He gave him a brief outline of what was intended, after which he left him to his reflections.

From that on he and his brother were busy packing what they intended taking with them. Dinner was served early, and the balance of the evening was spent by the Black Eagle coaching the Frenchman in the part he was to play.

He retired to his studio about eleven, in order to look up things, but at precisely midnight he returned to the lounge-hall to tell Sartel to get his things on.

The Frenchman went upstairs to obey, and the Black Eagle was pacing up and down, waiting for him to return, when the stillness of the place was shattered by the sound of the buzzer.

The Black Eagle strode across, and switched out the lights. Then he slid open the little panel which looked out into the porch, and saw a single blurred figure standing close to the door. It reminded him a little of the night Sartel had arrived, only on this occasion it was clear, crisp, and windless.

He closed the panel and pressed the light switch. As he did so, he saw Sartel just on the point of descending the stairs.

He motioned to him to remain where he was, and then, as his brother was still above, he went through the short lobby to open the door, for he thought it must be some urgent message from the garage; or, if it were not, he hadn't the slightest doubt that he would be able to take care of whomsoever it might be.

He swung open the door, and a man plunged through. He slid past the Black Eagle and, just inside the lounge, turned. As he did so the Black Eagle's eyes hardened to twin steel-like points, for he recognised, at first glance, Pierre Barat, one of the senior detectives of the Paris Surete.

And he knew in that same moment that Barat, single-handed, and without any assistance from Scotland Yard, must have picked up Sartel's trail on the coast of Brittany and, by no little ingenuity, had succeeded in tracking him straight through to the house of the Black Eagle in the crescent off the Edgware Road.

In less tense circumstances the Black Eagle could have found time to admire such a piece of work, but just now he had not even an academic interest in it. Nor was there time, for, as he turned, Barat flashed a heavy automatic.

"Put up your hands!" he snapped. "You will know why I have come here, and when I leave Sartel goes with me. Where is he?"

The Black Eagle would never have answered that question, but there was no need. The craven fool, Sartel, answered it himself. At sight of Barat, and at mention of his name, a loud gasp of fear had escaped him, and Barat, taking a single stride into the hall, looked up the staircase, and saw him shivering about midway up.

Momentarily, the man from the Surete had forgotten the Black Eagle, and that was a fatal thing to do.

The Black Eagle had nothing but contempt for Sartel. On the other hand, the sight of a man from the Surete was to him like a red rag to a bull, and, even as Barat turned, the Black Eagle's terrible hands came up.

He shot them out, and the long fingers gripped Barat by the throat. At the touch, the man from the Surete realised his danger. He gave a jump to get clear, and tried to turn to deal with this immediate menace.

But as he did so there came a crash from the direction of the stairway, and, as Barat slid limply through his hands, the Blank Eagle looked up to see Sartel standing with a smoking pistol wobbling in his podgy hand.

"You fool!" was all the Black Eagle said just then, as he looked down at Barat, whose twisted position told him all he needed to know.

HALF an hour after the killing of Barat a little procession passed through the lounge hall and went along a narrow passage that led to the rear of the house.

Before starting the Black Eagle had seen with his own eyes that every window had been fastened tight, the street door and the inner door of the lobby bolted and barred securely.

Sartel had stood whimpering beside the piece of clay which was his work. He had shuddered from touching it, but the menacing fingers of the Black Eagle's right hand on the back of his neck had steadied him.

"The last place in the world I would have had such a thing happen!" he snarled. "We don't know in whom Barat may have confided. There may be others who knew he was coming here. But, whether I like or no, I must help you now to get out of this country. If I fail, I shall have to kill you, in order to protect myself. So take him by the heels, and see that you do not falter."

And Sartel had obeyed.

The hunchback had taken the body by the shoulders, and, with the Black Eagle leading the way, they had reached a small lobby at the back of the house.

Here the Black Eagle opened a door and passed into a bricked passage not more than two feet wide.

He paused to take out a box of matches, and, striking one from time to time, led the way along for perhaps sixty paces or so, followed closely by the other two, with their burden.

The passage ended abruptly, but, after a cautioning gesture to Sartel, the Black Eagle allowed the match to go out, and pressed his hand at a certain spot in the wall.

Instantly there was a cold rush of air, and a long, narrow patch of something just verging out of blackness could be seen. The Black Eagle squeezed through the opening, and stood outside to receive the heels of the dead man. Sartel released them, and pressed through.

Then the body came along, with the hunchback still holding it under the armpits, and for the first time Sartel saw that a big black car was standing in a narrow lane which ran back of the high boundary wall of the garden. Opposite was the blank wall of a building of some sort.

The Black Eagle and his brother pushed the body into the back of the big limousine, and the hunchback got in.

Then the Black Eagle urged Sartel in after him. The former closed the door, but, peering through the window, Sartel could see him disappear through the slit in the wall.

Once inside the passage, the Black Eagle went along through the dark as certainly as he would have travelled had it been brilliantly lit.

He re-entered the house, and made his way to the lounge hall. Underneath the staircase was a low door, which, after taking out his keys, he unlocked. He had turned on a single light beneath the stairs, and by this was revealed a large metal tank which all but filled the cupboard which he opened.

He reached in, and turned a brass tap on the side; then he closed the door and relocked it.

Following that, he reached up and fumbled about with his fingers beneath the stairs, pressing gently on something which, had one taken the trouble to count, would have proved to be the seventh step from the bottom.

That done, he switched off the light and retraced his steps to the back of the house.

He locked the door after him, and, after slipping out into the lane, pulled the pivotal wall door after him. It closed as easily and as flush as the armour-plate door of a steel vault, and, had it been broad daylight, no passing soul would ever have guessed that it existed, so flush did it fit.

He strode to the car, and paused to speak a few low words to the driver. Then he opened the door and climbed in. The body was on the floor, while the hunchback was in one corner and Sartel in another.

As the Black Eagle began to pull down the blinds on one side, his brother did the same on his side, and the interior was entirely concealed from the gaze of anyone outside by the time they reached the Edgware Road.

Up that thoroughfare they sped, to the Marble Arch. Thence down Park Lane they went, and it was then the Black Eagle took something long and light-coloured from his pocket and tied it to the lapel of the dead man's coat.

Sartel watched, but did not dare ask what he was doing; nor did he notice that the Black Eagle's hands were gloved as he worked.

From Hyde Park Corner they drove down Constitution Hill until they rolled into the Mall. By this they reached the Admiralty Arch, and then the driver passed down Northumberland Avenue to the Embankment.

He turned to there, and just before he came to the Embankment side of New Scotland Yard he slowed down. As he did so he made a quick gesture with his head, and the next moment one of the two doors on the left-hand side of the limousine was opened.

The car travelled still more slowly, while something slid through the opened door and fell to the road; then at a tap on the glass the car gathered speed and the door closed. Inside there were now three living men, but the body of Pierre Barat was gone.

The car raced at high speed until it came to the Vauxhall Bridge. It turned on to that and crossed the river, swinging sharply to the left along the Wandsworth Road. It did not keep to that thoroughfare long, but turned soon into Nine Elms Lane and raced on into the Battersea Park Road.

By this it reached the Albert Bridge Road, and shot across the river again. Just across the bridge it turned recklessly to the right, once more striking the embankment on that side of the river, and as it tore along towards Chelsea Bridge it began to slow down.

About half-way between the two bridges it stopped, and, no sooner had it done so, than the Black Eagle jerked open the door and jumped out. He motioned for Sartel to follow, and, with one curt word to the driver, started across the pavement towards the wall.

His message had been brief and plain enough. This is how he received it from Abe Manstein.

"Half-way between the Albert Bridge and the Chelsea Bridge, on the Middlesex side, is a flight of steps leading down to the water. The gate which gives access to these steps will open at a touch, as the lock is broken. The tide will be high, but on the ebb. If you arrive there between a quarter-past one and half-past one you will find a boat waiting. Get in without saying a word. The men who man it have their instructions. They will not wait until after half-past one, as it is too dangerous and new plans will have to be made."

But the boat was there as arranged. The Black Eagle saw this as soon as he started down the steps. He reached the bottom and pushed Sartel over the side. He helped his brother to follow, and then he himself stepped in.

He could see that the craft was manned by four oarsmen, with a man in the stern sheets holding the tiller ropes. The moment he was in, a low sound came from the latter, and the boat shot away, making out into the middle of the river.

It seemed scarcely ten seconds later when, on the full sweep of the ebb, they rushed under the middle arch of Chelsea Bridge, and it was a curious coincidence that at that same moment a horrified constable was just discovering what lay close to the kerb, opposite the Embankment entrance to Scotland Yard.

*   *   *   *   *

It was just a little after eight o'clock in the morning when Detective-inspector Thomas, of Scotland Yard, rang the bell at the door of Sexton Blake's house in Baker Street.

Mrs. Bardell informed him that her master was still at breakfast, so the genial inspector made himself comfortable in the consulting-room in one of the low, saddlebag chairs, and with one of Blake's choicest Partagas between his strong, white teeth.

Blake and Tinker appeared a good half-hour later, and the former did not make any apology for keeping his visitor waiting. Their profession was such that a man must eat when he may, and that was quite understood between them. Blake sniffed the curling smoke of the cigar and smiled.

"I think I shall follow your example, inspector," he remarked pleasantly. "I had intended starting the day on an A-Batschari (the super-quality cigarette which Blake affected), but this box is too temptingly close."

The inspector either did not, or would not, see any strain of sarcasm in the words, for he grunted comfortably as he blew a fresh cloud of smoke into the air.

But when Blake had lighted up and was leaning back in his desk-chair, the man from the Yard came at once to the business which had brought him to Baker Street.

"Been reading about that affair in Paris?" he asked abruptly.

"You mean, I presume, the smash of the X— Bank?"

"Uh-huh!"

"Yes. Tinker, I believe, has clipped out what has appeared. What about it?"

"You know, then, that this feller, what's his name—one of the senior directors— cleared out with a big bunch of boodle, and was traced to Brittany?"

"Where he shot and killed two officials from the Paris Surete! Yes, I have read that,"

"Paris asked us, some days ago, to try and locate him over here, although it was generally thought he had tried to get through to Ireland by a fishing-smack from Brittany. We didn't really think he was in England—couldn't figure out how he could get past the watch we were keeping on all ports. But he is or, at least, it looks as if he was, after what happened last night. And I'll go on record now as saying that, for all the stone cold nerve, I've never seen anything to equal it."

"You interest me, inspector. What happened last night?"

"You know a good many of the men at the Surete. Did you ever meet one of the name of Pierre Barat?"

"Barat? Of course. I have worked with him. He was one of their ablest men. What has he to do with it? Did he have the case?"

"He did. And this is what has happened. He was murdered last night. Where, when, or how, I can't say; but shortly after one o'clock his dead body was found in the road immediately outside the Embankment entrance to Scotland Yard."

"Good heavens! Poor Barat! And outside the Yard. What else?"

"We don't know much yet. We have been through on the special telephone line to the Surete, and they have given us details of the record they have of Barat's movements up to the last they heard from him. That last came from Plymouth. It said that he had picked up the fugitive's trail in Brittany, and had certain proof that he had succeeded in making the coast of England. There were four fishing-boats which were reported delayed at sea during the gale of a week or so ago, and Barat pinned each of these outfits down as soon as they made port. I guess he must have put the screws on pretty heavily, but, at any rate, he evidently found out enough to convince him that his man had made for England, instead of Ireland.

"He mentions in his report that he had discovered other important information from one of Sartel's servants at his place on the Brittany coast, and it was this apparently that caused him to believe that his man was in England. He added that he had reason to believe that Sartel was making for a certain address in London, and he intended following him there. That is all the Surete had from him, and all they had heard about him until we 'phoned them that we had found his dead body just outside the Yard."

"Did he not put in his report the London address to which he believed Sartel was bound?"

"No. You see, after the killing of the other two men from the Surete, the Paris police were out for vengeance, Barat being one of their senior men, asked for and received the commission to track Sartel down. I have never met him personally, but it looks to me as if he was keeping a good deal of what he discovered to himself until he should lay his hands on his man. It would mean a big thing for him if he landed his fish alone, and we know from the papers that there is a big reward out for his capture."

"Um! What about his papers?"

"Nothing there. We found his Surete card, with full particulars of his identity and so on. There was a telegram in code, which he had received from the Surete while he was at Plymouth. Then a wallet containing French and English money, some, trinkets, his watch and chain, and, of course, his pistol, fully loaded, with a spare clip of cartridges in his hip-pocket."

"And that is all?"

"All except one thing—the most important of all. That is why I have kept it to the last. I will tell you what it was. Tied to the lapel of his coat—the left—was an ordinary plain manilla tag bearing some writing. What do you think that writing was? It was in French."

"Go on. It is too early in the morning to guess riddles."

"Well, I'll show it to you and you can see for yourself."

As he spoke the inspector drew something from the side pocket of his coat and passed it across to Blake. The latter took it, seeing as he did so, that it was just what the other had described—an ordinary plain manilla luggage label about five inches long by two and one half inches wide.

One side was perfectly blank, but the other bore writing in French. Blake laid it down and bent over it, and this is a rough translation of what his amazed gaze took in:

"My name is Pierre Barat, of the Paris Surete. Please ship me back to Paris, with the compliments of Scotland Yard."

That was all.

Blake looked up.

"I agree with you in saying that for stone cold nerve this takes a lot of beating, inspector. There is a nasty bit of business about this. And it strikes me as curious."

"How do you mean?"

"Why, in this way. If you have read the full history of the affair in Paris you must have gathered, as I did, that this fellow Sartel has shown up, as a pretty poor sort of fish, all the way through. It is not difficult to understand how, in a moment of panic, when he was run to earth in Brittany, he shot and killed the two men who had trailed him. Even a rat will fight a fox when it is cornered. But his whole record is that of a craven, and a person without very much moral fibre or depth of courage. Any assassin could have done what he did on that occasion. But this! This is a very different thing altogether."

"Well, who else would do it? Sartel was the man Barat was after, and he must have tracked him to the address which he had. But Sartel was too quick for him, and killed him just as he did the other two. In my opinion there is no other line to be drawn."

"You may be right. But why didn't Sartel indulge in some such pleasantry as this when he shot the other two? I don't say Sartel didn't kill Barat. But I do say that the man who wrote these words on this tag and tied it to the lapel of Barat's coat, had his nerve with him all right. And Sartel has not exhibited any such nerve as that would need.

"It isn't only a question of the tag. I don't think there is the slightest possibility that the killing took place near where the body was found."

"Of course not! It is too well patrolled. Why, hang it, Blake, he was found right at the entrance to the Yard."

"The patrol must have been slack for a few moments at any rate," returned Blake dryly. "But that is neither here nor there. What I am getting at is this. The tag was undoubtedly tied to the lapel after the killing. Barat would hardly be so obliging as to stand quietly whilst his assassin-to-be adorned him with this jeering message. Therefore, there would be no time for such business if he was killed near the Yard. But the fact remains that he was dropped off there shortly after, and that is the point I am getting at.

"I maintain that, if I have analysed Sartel's character anywhere near correctly, he would not possess the nerve to kill his man, adorn him with this tag containing an insulting jeer at Scotland Yard as well as the Surete and then deposit him at the very entrance to the Yard. Was nothing heard or seen? Who discovered him? And how long is it thought he was dead before he was found?"

"The constable on duty on the Embankment side found him. He

swears that he was absent from the entrance to the gate not more than ten or fifteen seconds on any single occasion. Between one o'clock and when he found Barat's body he was inside just once. He paced up the courtyard and paced back and, it was on his return, he saw something that looked like a bundle lying close to the kerb. He thinks that a car must have passed just then, for he could hear the sound of one dying away along the Embankment. As for how long he had been dead, the police surgeon thinks it could not have been much more than an hour."

"Well, why have you come to me about it?"

The inspector shifted uneasily.

"Well, I—well—"

But he was not allowed to finish, for at that moment the telephone bell shrilled, and Blake swung to lift the receiver. Both the inspector and Tinker could not help but hear what he said, and when the former caught the name of M. Dupuis, the Prefect of Police of Paris, he pricked up his ears.

Tinker, too, began to get interested, and while neither he nor the inspector could know what M. Dupuis was saying at the other end, it was not very difficult to piece together a good deal of the conversation from Blake's end of it which was something as follows:

Blake: "Yes, Monsieur Dupuis—Sexton Blake speaking—yes, I have read what has appeared in the papers—shocking affair—one of the inspectors from Scotland Yard is with me now—yes, he has just been telling me about it—no, I can't say that I have—I agree with you—oh! I did not know that was what you meant—that I should take up the case as well—act either independently or with the Yard here—that would be up to Scotland Yard, of course—oh! No, no, that —I knew Barat personally, as you are aware —I should be very glad to do anything in my power to bring his murderer to justice what's that? I didn't catch what you said— go across to Paris?—um—I could, of course, but—well, look here, Monsieur Dupuis, I will tell you what I will do—I will speak of it to the official from Scotland Yard, who is here now—if there is no objection, then I shall run across to Paris to-day—I could be there about ten to-night—shall we leave it at that—if I am not coming I shall send you a telegram—I will talk it over immediately and see what the opinion of my friend from Scotland Yard is—yes, if I come I shall bring a detailed report of in that is known—very well, monsieur, until then—au revoir—"

Blake hung up the receiver and turned round, looking at the inspector with a twinkle in his eyes.

"I suppose you gathered what that was," he remarked as he picked up the end of his cigar.

"That was easy enough," grunted Thomas. "So the prefect wants you to take up the case, eh?"

"With the approval and permission or Scotland Yard," rejoined Blake. "Would you object?"

"'Object' Of course we wouldn't object. He is at liberty to call in a private practitioner if he wishes. But what's eating him anyway? Does he think that bird Sartel is going to pull off a thing like this right under the windows of Scotland Yard and get away with it?"

"I am sure he has the utmost confidence in the ability of the Yard to track down Sartel," murmured Blake. "What he asked of me was that I should take an interest in the matter and try and run down the man who killed Barat."

"Does that mean you don't think Sartel did it?" exploded the inspector.

"Not at all, my dear fellow. He may or may not have killed Barat, but I am willing to wager you a five pound note here and now that Sartel is not the person who dumped Barat's body off in front of Scotland Yard."

"Whom could it have been, then? Answer me that? Sartel was working on his own, wasn't he? He had nerve enough to kill those other two men from the Surete, hadn't he?"

"Perfectly true. But I still maintain that Sartel did not possess sufficient nerve to do what was done last night, If he had, then all the things which have been written about him are mere journalistic ravings, and I do not think the whole of the journalistic profession in Paris is off the track to that extent,"

"Well, then, who killed him? Or, rather, who dumped him off at the Yard?

"My dear inspector, I don't know anymore than you. I haven't seen the body. I only know from what you have said that Barat was shot through the heart. I do not even know if a bullet was found in the body or not. So how can I advance a theory? But I will make one suggestion. Who was the person whose address in London Sartel was thought by Barat to possess? Where did this person live? And did Sartel reach him? If he did, was it while he was there that Barat was shot? Did Barat succeed actually in tracking Sartel to that place? If he did, then why shouldn't that other mysterious unknown have had a hand in the murder?

"But what motive? What could he have against Barat? Unless he had been mixed up in the looting of the bank with Sartel, what could he have against Barat?"

"All perfectly true, and probably correct. I just raised those questions in passing. But to get back to our muttons as our French friends say, have you any objection to my running across to see Monsieur Dupuis, and telling him all you have told me?"

"Certainly not!"

"Might I have a look at the body before I go?"

"Of course. I wanted you to come on there, anyway."

"Good! We can drive down in the Grey Panther. I think—"

But what it was he thought Blake did not say, for just then he broke off, and bent closer over the luggage label with which he had been idly toying. He held it this way and that, and finally he opened a small drawer, and took out a strong magnifying-glass.

The inspector and Tinker watched him, puzzled, while he studied the smooth surface of the manilla card. They saw him turn it over and examine the blank side, and, after that, hold it up to the light, as if to try and see through it.

Then he laid it down again, and once more held the glass over the side which bore the writing. At last he looked up.

"I'll tell you one thing about this card, inspector," he said thoughtfully. "It may be of some use to you. At any rate, you can use it if you wish."

"What is it?"

"Ingrained in the surface of this card is a big device, which is scarcely noticeable with the naked eye. It is the representation of a windmill, and I happen to know that such a watermark is one of the registered designs of one of the big Dutch paper mills. I should hazard a guess from this that this tag was manufactured in Holland, and, as there cannot be a very heavy import of this particular class of Dutch goods into England, it should not be an insoluble problem to discover through what importing house such tags are sold."

"Are you sure, Blake?"

"I am quite sure, unless the watermark is a forgery on the part of some pirate paper firm. And I'll tell you something else about it. This writing here—I do not believe it was written by Sartel, even if he tried to disguise his hand. It is not the caligraphy of a Frenchman, or of any Continental person. It was written by someone who learned the art either in this country or America. It is typically the hand of such a person. There are two tips to which you are perfectly welcome. And now, in return, may I ask a favour?"

The inspector did not look as if he attached very much value to the two "tips" which Blake had gratuitously handed him, but he nodded.

After all, Blake had put him in the way of many a good thing in the past, and it was entirely due to Blake that he had made the biggest coup of his whole career in the strange case which was unofficially referred to between them as that of "The Clue of the Four Wigs."

"What is it you want?"

"If I do go to Paris, may I take this card with me—just over one night?"

"Yes, if you attach so much importance to it."

"Oh, it isn't that, but—"

Blake rose without finishing his remark, and sent Tinker round to the garage for the Grey Panther.

He and the inspector talked of other things until the lad tooted at the kerb; then they passed out, and less than half an hour later Blake was standing with the police divisional surgeon over the body of poor Barat, the man from the Surete, who had been shot down so ruthlessly.

CHAPTER 6. A Warning to Sexton Blake—Sets of Finger-Prints—A Dramatic Crossing to Dieppe.

SEXTON BLAKE did not leave for Paris in the early afternoon, as he had intended. He was detained at Scotland Yard longer than he thought, and it was nearly two o'clock when he finally got back to Baker Street.

It was then that he came upon something that puzzled him considerably, and would certainly have disturbed the average citizen. It was a communication which had been pushed through the letter flap of the front door while he and Tinker had been at the Yard.

It was Tinker who had picked it up, but, seeing that it was marked "Private," he passed it to Blake. Blake opened it when he had thrown off his things and was seated at his desk.

As he grasped the contents, his eyes hardened and his jaw set. It was by no means the first time he had received a threatening letter. Indeed, such things were almost of daily occurrence at Baker Street, and, with very few exceptions, they were tossed into the wastepaper basket after a superficial glance.

But this one was worded somewhat differently from the great majority, and for that reason Blake read it carefully a second time. It ran thus:

"Sexton Blake.

"Sir,—It is known that an inspector from Scotland Yard visited you to-day. It is believed that his visit to you had reference to a certain incident which took place last night in the vicinity of Scotland Yard. The writer of this communication has received instructions that should you take any part whatsoever in this affair you do so at your peril.

"The officials at Scotland Yard will be dealt with in due course and without warning. But your case is different, and I am instructed to inform you that, while there may be some delay in bringing home to you that this is no idle threat, your fate will be as certain and as unpleasant as that of Barat. Your movements will be closely watched, and, clever as you profess to be, you will not discover the identity of those who watch you. The writer is being amply paid to pass on this warning to you, and your fate is in the hands of those who are quite competent to carry out instructions if you are so foolish as to disregard the warning. I am instructed to add that this is none of your affair, and that you are to KEEP OUT."

Blake tossed the communication across to Tinker.

"Read that, my lad," he said curtly. "Let me have your comments on it after lunch. Be careful of your fingers. This afternoon I want you to test it and the envelope for finger-prints. When you have finished reading it, put it away and come in to lunch."

With that he rose, and went along to the dining-room, where Mrs. Bardell was just serving lunch. Tinker joined him a few minutes later, and when the housekeeper had retired the lad said:

"It's a queer letter, guv'nor. What do you make of it?"

"I told you to let me have your comments first."

"Well, sir, did you notice that the bird who wrote it said several times that he was acting under instructions?"

"That is exactly what I wanted to know if you noticed. In that respect it is somewhat different from the usual effusions that we receive. It is almost a blend of the first person and the third person."

"Yes, sir, I saw that. And near the end he doesn't disguise that it is the Barat affair that he is referring to."

"No. Which, to my mind, my lad, further strengthens my contention that there is more than the bank thief, Sartel, behind the killing of Barat.. Sartel is a fugitive from French justice. If I have sized that situation up anything near like correct, then I imagine Sartel's mind is exercised by one all-consuming idea—to put as many leagues between himself and the Paris Surete as he can. I do not believe for a single moment that he has the time, the nerve, the desire, or the mental capacity to jazz about London in such fashion, deliberately baiting Scotland Yard and the Surete, making it perfectly obvious that he is here, and, to use a vulgar expression, thumbing his nose at them as if daring them to catch him. Sartel is not the type to do that. That is why I say there must be someone else mixed up in the business."

"You mean in that bank scandal, guv'nor?"

"Not necessarily. As far as we can gather Sartel was playing a lone hand until he struck England. But I am convinced that he is not doing so now. However, we shall not say anything about that to Inspector Thomas just at present. He seems a little peeved with me as it is, so we will let him sweat for a bit."

"And the letter, guv'nor?"

Blake shrugged.

"We shall treat that as we treat them all; only, we shall preserve this one in case it may be of use. Make a very careful examination of the writing and the surface. Take dust impressions of any finger-prints and photograph them. Also, don't forget the watermark. It looked to me like very ordinary paper that could be bought at any stationer's, but you never can tell.

"It must have some meat behind it, for the writer certainly guessed correctly why Inspector Thomas came here this morning. Which goes to prove that whoever is behind this Barat affair is not leaving any loose threads sticking out; and, moreover, for some reason or other, is determined to keep us out of the business if he can. What his reason for that may be we can't even guess. But if you get a chance I think it would be as well to look up the whereabouts of as many of the master crooks of our acquaintance as possible—those who are not in prison."

"Well, we know where one is, anyway," remarked Tinker, after a pause.

"Whom do you mean, young Un?"

"Why, the Black Eagle. At least we know where he was last Thursday when we came back from Harwich."

Blake had been looking at Tinker while the lad was speaking, and now he kept on staring at him, but in an unseeing way. His eyes were fixed as if his whole mental process had been suddenly arrested, and for a full minute or more he did not alter his pose.

Then he seemed to come back to the present and resumed his lunch without making any reply to Tinker's last remark.

After lunch Tinker betook himself to the laboratory, where he settled down to make a thorough examination of the anonymous letter for finger-prints.

The lad was really an expert in such matters, for, aside from the training he had received under Blake, he had put in a good many long hours of study at Scotland Yard, where there is probably the most extensive library of finger-prints and paraphernalia relating there is in existence.

In the meantime Blake again gave his attention to the manilla luggage label, which had been found tied to the lapel of Barat's coat.

He brought into play the most powerful magnifying glass he possessed and went over each detail of the faint, whitish watermark with the utmost care.

At last he found one little additional trademark worked into the device of the windmill, which convinced him that the tag had actually been manufactured by the big Dutch paper-mill of which he had spoken to Inspector Thomas, and not by some pirate mill that had forged the watermark.

When he felt satisfied of this, he rang through for a messenger boy and, while waiting, wrote out a telegram addressed to the office of the mill in question.

He had taken care to secure their address in Amsterdam from a trade directory on one of the shelves in the Consulting-room. He sent this off "urgent," and then applied himself to cleaning up certain arrears of work, which he wished to finish before leaving for Paris.

He had already given up all idea of catching the afternoon train, and was now figuring on making the eight-twenty in the evening from Victoria.

It was just before tea-time that Tinker appeared, looking pretty grubby from the black dusting powder which he had been using, and the chemicals he had employed in the dark-room when developing his negatives.

He had a dozen or so wet prints in his hand, which he handed to Blake, one by one, commenting on each as he did so. Blake, with a magnifying glass in his hand, received them, and studied them as the lad talked.

"There are five distinct types altogether," said the lad. "I have made two prints of each and two of a blurred mass, which might have been caused by two or more fingers resting on the same spot. The paper is, as you thought, just an ordinary bit of cheap notepaper, which can be purchased at any stationer's.

"It is watermarked with a lion and, in the watermark record book in the laboratory, I find that such a device is used by five different British paper-mills. They all vary in form more or less, and this one belongs to the Atlas Mill.

"Now, sir, those first two prints—if you will study the whorls and the outer lines you will see that they are much finer and, in a way, more delicate than any of the others. I place them as those of a woman and I figure they might have been made by a girl-clerk in the stationer's, where the paper was bought. If that is so, then the sheet which we have must have been the outside one of the packet. If I am wrong, then they were made by someone who handled the paper after it was bought."

"Well theorised, my lad. Go on."

Tinker flushed a little at the praise; then he grinned boyishly.

"The second set, guv'nor, is not so good. The two prints are undoubtedly from the same finger, or, rather, I should say one is a finger and one the thumb. I found them each on one side of the paper, one superimposed, as you would say, over the other, which is practically all the proof we need that they were made when someone held the sheet of paper between thumb and finger—in the case the first finger I should think. I can't even guess who might have made them.

"Thirdly, we have these other two. They are not very good, but, as far as I can make out, one was made by the same person who made those in set two, and one by the bird who was responsible for those in set four, which is here.

"This fourth set is the best of the lot and you will see is almost as delicate in outline as set one. But while I think set one was made by a woman, I do not think a woman was responsible for set four. On the other hand, it is my opinion that it was made by a man of small stature. The measurements fit in with scale number six in our measurement book, and following up the tables relating to that, it would mean, if all the other figures are correct, they were made by a man just a little over five feet in height—say, anything between five feet and five feet four inches.

"There is just one last point about set four which I want to mention before showing you the last copies. You see, those tiny little marks along the inner whorls?"

Blake nodded as he laid the magnifying glass over what Tinker referred to.

"Well, sir, do you remember telling me once that such tiny spots had never been found in the finger-prints of any of the pure Nordic races?"

"I do."

"Aren't those the sort of almost invisible spots you meant?"

"They certainly are, my lad."

"Then they were caused from an excessive number of sweat pores in the skin, which, according to you, are possessed by some Eastern races, but not by pukka Europeans."

"That's the stuff, Tinker. What else?"

"That's all except that I figure that the person who made those prints was perspiring considerably at the time he held that sheet of paper in his hand and, as it is cold weather at present, he must have been in a very warm room or in a nervous state when the print was made."

Blake laid down the prints and looked up.

"My lad," he said quietly, "I couldn't have given a better little lecture on these than that. You seem to have covered every possible point, and I don't disagree with even a fraction of it. What are the last two?"

"Nothing much, guv'nor. Just two blurs, but I thought I'd include them while I was at it."

Blake glanced at them, then he handed the whole lot back to the lad.

"You can spend a quiet evening at Scotland Yard with those," he remarked. "I am crossing to Paris to-night on the eight-twenty from Victoria. You can drive me to the station in the Grey Panther and go on to the Yard from there. Get hold of one of the men in the fingerprint department and see if you can locate anything similar to these among their records."

"Very good, sir."

Blake had no difficulty in getting a seat on the evening train, and on reaching Newhaven went at once on board. He was by no means unmindful of the anonymous letter which he had received, and both he and Tinker had kept a sharp look-out from the time they left Baker Street for any signs that they were being shadowed.

They had, however, seen nothing to rouse their suspicions, nor did Blake spot anyone among the crowd boarding the boat who looked as if he might be there for some nefarious purpose. But then, Blake reflected, appearances very seldom counted.

He went down to the saloon as soon as they left harbour and ate a light supper, for he had already dined before leaving Baker Street. He sipped a whisky-and-soda, and then, lighting a cigar, made his way up on deck for a stroll and a smoke before trying to get some sleep before reaching Dieppe.

It was just getting on for midnight when he stepped out on to the deck, and he knew that they must be just about half-way across. There was scarcely another soul to be seen, for the night was chilly and the Channel pretty rough.

But that did not discommode Blake, so turning up the collar of his overcoat he began a brisk promenade. Up and down he went, then, to vary it, crossed from time to time to the other side of the deck, and continued his walk there.

It was on one of these occasions, when he was pacing up and down the port side that he happened to glance over the side, and, some distance up Channel, saw the lights of a steamer of some sort coming down.

He watched her idly for a little, and then grew more interested as he saw another pair of lights suddenly appear and grow closer and closer to those of the first craft.

It was impossible at that time of night to make even a hazard at how far they were from each other, but, as he could see it, it looked to Blake as if the newcomer was heading rather dangerously close to the other.

Then the latter appeared to swing round, for one of her lights disappeared from view, and, a few minutes later, Blake saw the lights of the second almost blend with the one visible gleam on the first. He rubbed his chin thoughtfully.

"That's kind of odd," he muttered. "If it didn't seem an extraordinary thing to do at midnight in the Channel I would almost say that those two craft were hove to, and that some business was going on between them. But it is probably just an optical delusion of the water at night."

He dismissed the matter then, and continued his promenade, but he little dreamed how correct he had been. And certainly he would have been much more deeply interested if he had known that there was business being transacted between those two craft which, as he had suspected, were indeed hove to, and that the business was nothing less than the transfer of the Black Eagle, Sartel, and the Black Eagle's brother from one ship to the other. Captain Gemeaker had kept his rendezvous to the minute.

Blake then went below to lie down, but as soon as the steward touched him on the shoulder he was awake. He returned to the deck to find that they were just entering Dieppe Harbour.

Being an old hand at the cross-Channel game he made his way to where he knew the gangway would be, and stood there ready to be one of the first ashore.

Soon other passengers began to gather, and by the time they were warping into the dock there was a hundred or so bunched up at that part of the deck, all pushing and jamming as if their very lives depended on their being among the first to get ashore.

Blake had found a convenient stanchion against which he was leaning, thus keeping back the human wall which threatened to drive him over the rail. And he was in that position when at last the gangway was hauled aboard.

At that, as if it were a signal, the mob swayed forward again, and it was just then that Sexton Blake felt something plunge in under his arm, along his side, and then stop as a heavy blow caught him just under the short rib.

The force of the impact drove him forward, and he almost went down as the crowd milled about him. He recovered himself and turned savagely to reprimand the person who had been so violent. But just as he did so something dropped to the deck at his feet, arresting him.

He managed to elbow his nearest neighbours aside sufficiently to enable him to crouch down and pick up what had fallen.

As his fingers encountered the object they closed on it, and he rose. As he did so he allowed the object to slip into his outside coat pocket, and then he turned, and, under the glare of the powerful electric light which had been lit at the head of the gangway, he coolly and deliberately studied every face within his range of vision.

But there was nothing there to tell him who was the person who had tried to murder him under cover of the crowd. So much shifting had there been that he might still be close at hand, or he might be one of two score or more who were jammed up together within a radius of a dozen feet.

But attempted murder it had been as Sexton Blake felt his side and found the cloth of his heavy travelling coat cut clean through. Attempted murder with a more than ordinarily vicious determination behind it, for the blow which had struck him had had all the weight of the would-be assassin behind it, and the object he had picked up from the deck was a knife with a blade no less than twelve inches long.

CHAPTER 7.   Sexton Blake's Arrival at the Paris Surete—Prince Menes and Madame Goupolis.

WHO was it among that crowd that had tried to assassinate him? As far as he knew he had never before seen a single soul among his fellow-passengers. What could have been the motive? Was it someone who had tried to carry out the threat which had been contained in the anonymous letter which arrived at Baker Street that day?

Blake allowed himself to be swept down the gangway, and then he hurried along to the customs shed, where he soon found the porter who had taken his bag on ahead. He finished there without the formality of opening his bag, for he showed the special card from the Paris Surete which he always carried when in France.

Then he sent the porter on with the bag to secure a seat for him while he hurried through to the bureau of the passport official whose desk each passenger must pass before being allowed to board the train.

In a few words Blake explained who he was, again showing the card from the Surete. He added that he wished, if possible, to be placed in such a way that he could scrutinise each passenger as he or she stood to have his or her passport stamped.

The official was most obliging, and just as the first of the crowd began to come along from the customs shed he found himself thrust behind a screen where, somewhat to his surprise, he discovered a Secret Service man standing also making a secret surveillance of the passengers as they came along.

The screen was provided with two or three little peepholes, quite invisible to those who were passing beyond the passport desk, and through one of these Blake was able to watch without fear of detection.

But all to no purpose. There was a dozen; there was none. He saw no face that he had not seen at Newhaven. When the last laggard had hastened by, Blake had a short conversation with the Secret Service man, and from him he gleaned the information that among the lot he had marked down three Communist suspects about whom he was telegraphing to Paris.

Blake told him what had happened just before he landed, showing him the long rent in the side of his coat, and the knife which he had picked up from the deck. The Secret Serviceman was all for making a complete canvass of the whole train, interrogating each and every passenger; but Blake would not allow it.

"No, monsieur," he said as he thanked the man. "In my profession as in yours such an incident is not unusual. I shall take good care that if another attempt is made I shall deal with the fellow as he deserves."

And here he drew out and revealed for a moment the butt of his heavy automatic. "I shall, of course, mention the matter to Monsieur Dupuis on my arrival in Paris, but I do not wish the trainload of passengers disturbed. If it should happen to be one of those you have marked down as 'suspect,' then I have no doubt your colleagues in Paris will soon ferret him out on some other charge and deal with him."

He made his way to the train then, but all the way to Paris he took good care to keep his automatic handy, even though he was travelling in a private reserved compartment which the stationmaster had insisted on placing at his sole disposal.

On reaching the Gare St. Lazare, Blake found, somewhat to his surprise, that Monsieur Dupuis, the Prefect, had taken the trouble to come himself to meet him, which, at the early hour of half-past five in the morning, was a thing to be appreciated.

He was accompanied by two inspectors from the Surete—friends and colleagues of the late Barat.

They all drove in the Prefect's car direct to the Ile de la Cite, where Blake was accommodated in Monsieur Dupuis' private apartment. He breakfasted there, and afterwards he and the Prefect settled down to discuss the Barat affair.

Monsieur Dupuis first produced Sartel's police dossier, and this Blake studied carefully. When he had finished, he listened to what the Prefect had to say, waiting until he had finished before putting any questions.

Then he, in his turn, gave a full report of all he had been able to glean at Scotland Yard, winding up by producing the manilla luggage label which had been found tied to the lapel of Barat's coat.

As Blake explained this, the prefect's eyes glinted with sudden anger. He had not yet heard about that from Scotland Yard. He read the impudent and insulting message, then he turned to Blake.

"What do you make of this, monsieur?"

Blake gave him a resume of his deductions much as he had given to Tinker and Inspector Thomas. He explained why he did not believe that Sartel had had the nerve to carry out such a piece of impudent work, and, the prefect nodded his agreement;

"You are right, M. Blake. Sartel—he would never do such a thing, because he could not. From his dossier you will see the sort of creature he was—a poor, weak fool of a boulevardier, with no backbone, as you English put it, and as putty in the hands of a clever woman. Besides, this is not the writing of a Frenchman. The calligraphy is not of this country."

"That is the conclusion I myself came to, monsieur, and that is why I asked the inspector from Scotland. Yard to permit me to bring the card across to show you. Have you specimen's of Sartel's writing?'

"One of my men will have. I shall ring for him and get it."

He pressed a button, and an orderly appeared. He gave the man certain instructions, and a few minutes later one of the inspectors who had been at the Gare St. Lazare entered. The prefect told him what he wished, and the man hastened out to return a few moment's later with a thick leather portfolio.

From this he selected certain sheets of paper which he handed to his chief. The prefect passed them to Blake, and the latter saw at first glance, on comparing the writing with that on the luggage label, that they were utterly different in every way.

Blake himself was, of course, an expert in handwriting, that science being one of the most important adjuncts to his profession.

But nevertheless, he wanted an independent opinion on the matter, so, as he handed the sheets of paper back, he asked if one of the experts at the Surete could make an examination of the two specimens, and let them have a report soon. The prefect readily agreed, and the inspector took the card away with the others.

Then Blake approached a phase of the matter which he had kept until the last, but which, from the very first moment when he had read of Sartel's embezzlement, had been in the back of his mind.

"This woman who was mixed up in the affair," he said, "from your words M. Dupuis, and from what I have read, it seems that Sartel was greatly under her influence."

The prefect snorted.

"Monsieur Blake, Sartel was the woman's slave. He was worse. Until he fell into her toils he was neither better nor worse than the average. He was a mediocre man in his profession, and had been pushed up into the position he occupied by family and political influence. But from the moment he met that woman he was as putty in her hands. I am convinced that it was for her he first began to cook matters at the bank, and at last found himself in so deep that he had to run for it.

But when that moment came the woman would have none of him. How much she managed to squeeze out of him I cannot say, but I believe she got away with a big sum. And she has got entirely clear, I am sorry to say. We haven't a single hope of catching her until she is again tempted out of her present place of hiding."

Blake knit his brows. He was a little puzzled at this.

"I don't quite follow what you mean," he said. "I take it she has escaped from France. But isn't it possible to have her arrested if you know where she is?"

The prefect shrugged, and spread out his hands.

"She is in Egypt, monsieur, and unfortunately is now under the protection of an Egyptian prince who is too powerful for us in his own country. The Egyptian government dares not touch him."

"I know one such prince in Egypt," remarked Blake slowly. "His name is Menes —Prince Menes. Is it he by any chance?"

"Monsieur, you have named the man!"

Blake sat up suddenly.

"That woman, monsieur, is she by any chance a Greek woman, do you know?"

"I have discovered only within the last three days that she is supposed to be Greek, Monsieur Blake."

"And can you tell me if one of her names is Goupolis?"

"Monsieur, you have again named it. What do you know of her?"

"Plenty—plenty! Pardon me, Monsieur Dupuis. I want a few minutes to think. This that you have just told me puts an entirely different complexion on one phase of the case."

For ten minutes Blake paced up and down the prefect's private bureau, his mind working at high pressure over the amazing discovery that Madame Goupolis was the woman who had been mixed up with Sartel in the bank scandal. To Blake it was all too clear now how she would find little difficulty in making Sartel her creature.

She had done it some years before with Jules Vabour, and she was still beautiful enough and evil enough to repeat the trick. But it opened up an entirely new channel of thought which he was not yet ready to share with the prefect, so, when finally he sat down he said:

"You asked me to do what I can to help in running down this man, Sartel, monsieur, I was undecided until a few minutes ago. But now I can give you my answer."

"And that is, M. Blake?"

"It is 'yes.' Sartel is, as we suspect, not the only person mixed up in the death of Barat. I was of that opinion before leaving London, and I am still more strongly convinced that I am right. I have a suspicion a very faint suspicion, monsieur, which I shall try to trace to something definite. In order to do that I must return to England without delay. Every hour is precious now, if what I think should prove solid enough to hold water, so to speak. I cannot say more now but you may rest assured that I shall do all in my power to discover the truth, and will, of course, advise you fully the very first possible moment."

The prefect held out his hand. "Monsieur Blake, I am most grateful and content to receive your news when you feel disposed to give it. I know that if any living man can enable us to avenge Barat, you are that man."

And thus it was that Sexton Blake hastened back to London that same afternoon, making the journey in just a trifle over two hours by special aeroplane from Le Bourget to Croydon.

CHAPTER 8. The House of Mystery—Silence and Darkness.

BLAKE found Tinker at work in the consulting-room when he walked in. He had not telegraphed the lad how he was coming, and when he announced that he had come by air, Tinker was somewhat peeved that he had not been permitted to run down to Croydon in the Grey Panther.

But he soon forgot his momentary disappointment by the time Blake had finished with what he had to say. First, however, he asked the lad what luck he had had at Scotland Yard the night before.

"Nothing doing," Tinker informed him. "I guess we covered the whole bag of tricks, but we couldn't match any of them."

"Um. Well, it will have to wait. I had quite an interesting visit with the prefect in Paris, and discovered one rather important thing."

"What was that, guv'nor?"

"You remember reading in the papers that there was a woman mixed up in the bank frauds with Sartel?"

"Yes, sir."

"Well, that woman was our old friend, Madame Goupolis."

"The Greek dame! I thought France was too hot for her to risk going there."

"She risked it at any rate, and, from what the prefect tells me, it looks as if she cleaned up a nice bunch of stuff through Sartel. More than that she has got clean away with her share, for she is back in Egypt under the protection of Prince Menes."

"Which means she is as safe as houses? while she sticks there."

"Quite right."

Blake glanced at the clock; then he sat down at his desk.

"It is just half past six. We shall dine early, my lad. I have an expedition on foot for this evening?"

"Does that include me?" asked Tinker anxiously.

"It does—you and I alone."

"Then I am satisfied. What is the big idea?"

"You know the house in the crescent off the Edgware Road to which you followed the Black Eagle last Thursday."

"You bet."

"That is our destination."

"You mean we are going to call on him?"

"We are going to call on him if he is at home; we are going to have a look at the interior of his house if he is not at home. It may be necessary to do a little housebreaking, but we shall risk that if necessary."

"Now this business begins to look up a little," remarked Tinker in a tone of deep satisfaction. "But why are we going there, guv'nor? Is he mixed up in this business?"

"I haven't an idea, but I have some suspicions which I am going to put to the test if possible. Listen, my lad! You remember when we saw the Black Eagle at Parkstone Quay, at Harwich, last week?"

"Yes, sir."

"Well, he landed from the boat which had just come across from the Hook of Holland which means he had been in Holland. We have no means of knowing whether he was just returning to England after a long absence—since before that affair in Egypt to be exact—or whether he had been here for some time and had made just a brief visit to the Continent. If the latter, then we can't tell how long he has been lying low; but if the former, then it is not at all impossible that he was mixed up with Madame Goupolis in Paris in the Sartel affair. Do you follow me?"

"Yes, sir."

"I may be entirely wrong, but we do know that he has worked with the Greek woman on more than one occasion in the past, and might easily have had a hand in this last game of hers. And we know, too, that Sartel was trying to get to England in order to reach someone in London who, he thought, could help him to escape. That was plain enough from the notes which Barat forwarded to the Surete.

"But it was not what Monsieur Dupuis told me that first brought the Black Eagle into my mind. It was one of your remarks."

"Which one, guv'nor?"

"Yesterday, at lunch, when I mentioned casually that it might be a good idea to try and locate as many master crooks as possible and you replied that we knew, at least, where to find the Black Eagle. It was that and the luggage label which was found tied to the lapel of Barat's coat."

"I don't understand."

"Don't you recall that I pointed out to Inspector Thomas that the luggage label was of Dutch manufacture?"

"Wow!, I've got it now, guv'nor. You think it might have been a spare one which the Black Eagle brought across from Holland with him."

"Just that. It is only a wild supposition at best, but since then the other things I have come upon rather tend to strengthen that theory than to weaken it. And, at any rate, I am still convinced that Sartel, the craven, never had the nerve to tie on that label and dump Barat's body off in front of Scotland Yard. But the Black Eagle would have sufficient and to spare."

Tinker was thoughtful for a few minutes. Then:

"And that anonymous letter, guv'nor, do you think that came from the Black Eagle?"

"If he is working with Sartel, then it is quite on the cards that he inspired that letter even if he did not write it. It is not difficult for the Black Eagle to command the services of a small army of crooks. He is a rich man and he pays well for services rendered. And, incidentally, if it was one of his agents who tried to knife me as I was getting off the boat at Dieppe, I should like very much indeed to meet him face to face. At any rate, we shall pay him a visit after dinner."

This was the first Tinker had heard of the attempt on Blake's life, and nothing would do but that Blake must tell him all about it. But Blake reserved that until they were at dinner, and as soon as the meal was over they made their preparations to visit the house in the crescent.

In view of the fact that they did not know whether they should find the place tenanted or not, Blake prepared accordingly. They both donned suits of a nondescript dark cloth, and changed their ordinary shoes for rubber-soled "sneakers."

Dark flannel shirts with self-coloured collars attached, and dark-grey ties completed their outward attire, with the exception of dark grey caps having each a long peak which would pull well down over the eyes.

Needless to say, each provided himself with a loaded automatic and electric torch, and, in addition, Blake tucked into an inner pocket a small oiled-silk portfolio containing a beautifully fashioned, complete set of burglary and safe-breaking tools. These had been manufactured by hand by a certain specialist in that business who carried on his trade in a small village about fifty miles north of London, where he was looked upon as a highly respected blacksmith—one of the few remaining artisans of the old school who could still find a ready market for hand-wrought iron work.

It is a fact that the equipment had cost Blake no less than a thousand pounds, and, to-day, the outfit would cost five hundred more than that, as any high-class crib-cracker will tell one.

Just two other items completed Blake's preparations. One was a bunch of skeleton keys to which had also been attached the marvellous little flexible steel "spider" of his own invention. As an instrument for controlling the most complicated of locks that little "spider" was unsurpassed, and, so far as Blake knew, it was still an unknown quantity in the criminal world, as he intended to keep it. The other was a thin, but very strong, ladder made of twisted silk, with two hooks at one end.

They did not start out until it was full dark. Nor did they take a taxi, but, instead, walked leisurely from Baker Street to Oxford Street and along that thoroughfare to the Marble Arch, where they turned into the Edgware Road. They continued along this until they came to the short street leading into the crescent where the house of the Black Eagle was situated. They turned into this and, just as they were entering the crescent, met the constable on the beat.

That individual had already been regarding them suspiciously, and his attitude did not change when Blake first drew up and addressed him.

"Just take a walk back into the crescent, will you, officer," said Blake. "I want a word with you, and it is a little too public here."

"What's the game?" asked the constable gruffly. "Can't you say what you want to say here?"

Blake smiled.

"I could, Barrow, but I'd rather not."

At the mention of his name, the constable peered full into Blake's face; then he gave a sheepish grin.

"Sorry, sir; I didn't know it was you. Certainly, Mr. Blake, I'll come along with you. Nothing wrong, I hope?"

"Not at all," Blake assured him. "I just want a little information, if you can give it."

They walked into the crescent, which appeared to be entirely deserted, and when they were well in the shadow Blake drew up.

"That house over there on the corner, Barrow," he said. "Do you know if it is occupied at present?"

The constable turned and gazed at the high front wall of the house which had been built by the eccentric artist of the middle fifties of last century. With the exception of the single semi-circular window high up, the whole front face of the building was without a window. Then he looked back at Blake.

"I don't know, sir. There was someone in there a few days ago, for I remember seeing the light in that front window. It isn't often I see it. Whoever lives there— an artist man, I understand—doesn't seem to spend much time in it."

"I know that. Can you recall, Barrow, the last time you saw it? It is rather important to me to know."

Barrow scratched his chin and set his mind to work. He looked at the pavement and then at the house; then he studied the pavement again, and at last he glanced at Blake.

"Well, Mr. Blake, I wouldn't want to take my oath on it, but I'd say it was either Friday or Saturday night. I think it was Saturday."

"No chance of it being Sunday—last night?"

"No, sir. I wasn't on duty last night. I am almost sure it was the night before last."

"You haven't seen it to-night?"

"No, sir."

"Thank you Barrow. Tinker and I are going on there to pay a visit to the occupant if he is at home. That is why I wanted to know. I had an idea he might have gone away."

"Perhaps he has, sir, if there hasn't been a light. Maybe he is out of town for the week-end."

"That is an idea worth considering," returned Blake carelessly. Then: "We shall probably see you on our return, Barrow. Thank you for the information."

With that he nodded and started on, and Barrow, after hesitating for a few moments as if debating whether to follow or not, decided to continue on his beat, for he knew that in the next street there was a little packet of supper waiting for him at a certain house where the young woman he was to marry in the spring was in service as cook.

That was a mistake on Barrow's part. He might have shared in something quite interesting.

Blake and Tinker turned the corner where the strange house stood, and walked on to the deep, narrow porch which was the only visible outward means of access to the place. They plunged into the gloom here, and Blake at once pressed his finger on the bell button.

Standing close to the door they could hear the faint sound of the buzzer in the interior, but although he pressed again and again and again, no one came in answer to the summons.

For a last time Blake put his finger on the button, and kept it there a full two minutes or more. Still nothing happened, so at that he desisted.

"We seem to have drawn a blank," he muttered. "Let us have a look at the back."

They slipped out of the porch and made their way along the high brick wall until they came to the corner of a narrow lane, which, as Blake knew from having visited the place on a previous occasion, led simply to another blank wall at the end.

The alley was no thoroughfare, being part of the property of the house on the corner, although it would have been difficult for the uninitiated to figure out just why it had been arranged in that fashion by the original builder.

They entered the lane, where they were immediately swallowed by the gloom. The high wall continued on here as along the street, and, looking up, Blake saw that it was a good fifteen feet from where they stood to the top.

Just across was the blank face of another building containing no windows, and, as there had been no signs of any passers-by, it looked as if they might be able to work without being disturbed if they acted with sufficient caution.

Having failed at the door, it was Blake's intention to proceed with his alternative plan, for he felt pretty sure by now that the Black Eagle was not at home. But it was going to be no easy matter to surmount that wall. He might have tried to pick the lock of the door which they had just left, but he was too wise to attempt that.

He gave the Black Eagle credit for being far too shrewd to leave such a spot vulnerable to the attack of anyone who chose to investigate it during his absence.

And in that he was right, for the outer door, as well as the inner, had been doubly secured by heavy iron bars, which no housebreaking tools could shift, for inside the conventional wood panels of the doors were, in addition, heavy plates of steel.

Under ordinary circumstances that fifteen-foot wall would have presented a considerable problem, but Blake had had it in mind when making his preparations. And now, with Tinker on guard at the mouth of the alley, he set to work.

He took the silk ladder from under his waistcoat, where he had wound it round and round his body, and, when it was free, grasped it by the iron hooks while he collected most of the slack in the same hand.

Then he stood back, and a moment later the iron hooks shot upward as he threw with practised aim. But a moment later it came tumbling down again, and he muttered a soft imprecation as he made ready for a second throw.

It was just at that moment Tinker slid in through the gloom to whisper that someone was coming along from the crescent, so the pair flattened themselves down at the base of the wall close to the ground.

Whoever the pedestrian was, he chose to pause just at the mouth of the alley, and for a second or so they thought he was coming in. But then a match flared, and they saw he was only lighting a cigarette. He passed on when he had thrown the match away, and Tinker slid along to resume his watch, while Blake again prepared for the throw.

This time he was successful. The hooks caught on the top of the wall, and he tested them with his full weight. He gave a low hissing sound which brought Tinker back, and then, with a whispered word to the lad, Blake began to mount.

He went up easily, while Tinker held the lower part of the ladder out so as to make it easier for Blake to get a toehold, and then the tension suddenly slackened as Blake reached the top and straddled it.

Tinker next essayed to climb, and in a few seconds he was sitting beside Blake.

"I don't know what is down here," whispered Blake, "but I fancy a garden of sorts. But we shall not drop here. I am going along the wall towards the corner. I can't understand what that heavy black shadow is that runs right along the top of the street wall from the corner to the house. Follow me, and if anyone comes along the street, lie as flat as you can until they pass."

Blake had rolled up the ladder while he spoke, and now, thrusting it into the side pocket of his coat, he began shinnying along, with Tinker close behind him.

They had only a short distance to go, not more than twenty feet in all, and it had been due to the light from a lamp in the street beyond that Blake had spotted the long, black shadow which, had puzzled him.

And he was almost upon it before he discovered what it was. He paused, and turned his head.

"It is solid brick," he whispered, "About two feet wide. I wonder— I think I have it, Tinker. The wall here is, apparently, that thick, but I don't believe it. I'll wager that it is a double wall with a secret passage in between. If it is, it will explain how the Black Eagle could get in and out of the house, without using the door on the street. It will only be a waste of time to try and investigate it from the outside. But we might be able to learn the secret when we are inside. I am going to drop the ladder here close beside it. Be ready to follow me down."

With that, Blake took the silk ladder from his pocket and allowed it to uncoil inside the wall. He hooked the iron hooks over the top, and then swung round to descend. He slid rather than climbed down, and as soon as he felt the tension slacken, Tinker followed.

At the bottom there was some delay until Blake managed to shake the hooks off the top, but they came tumbling down at last, and again he stuffed the ladder into the side pocket of his coat.

He touched Tinker's arm before they advanced.

"Get your pistol where you can reach it quick," he whispered. "Also, have your torch handy, but, do not use it until I give the word. I will guide us with mine along this wall. And watch your step. We don't know what we may strike before we are through with this. The house may be in darkness, and no one may answer the bell, but that is no criterion that the place is empty."

Then Blake started forward, but if he had guessed for a single moment what they were to encounter in that dark, silent house of mystery, even he might have paused.

CHAPTER 9. Investigations in the Mysterious House—The Creeping Death

BY the light of Blake's torch they reached a heavy door set in the back of the house close to the brick wall which they had been following. Before attempting to force a way through, Blake followed the side of the house to the right until he came to the corner, and turned to the left there.

In this way they carried on, until they again reached a high brick wall, which they knew must shut the place off on the crescent side. But while they could see windows above them, there was no sign of another door. Nor did they see the gleam of a single light on that side.

So they retraced their steps until they were back once more at the heavy door, which they could see by the torch had been painted a dark green.

A cursory examination revealed that, on the outside, it was fitted with a heavy wrought-iron handle and two brass lock-plates—one about three feet from the bottom sill, and one the same distance from the top.

The keyholes were mere slits, and Blake recognised that at once as a very special and exceedingly complicated form of lock, which had just come on the market.

He had never attempted to force one of them with the "spider," but now he set to work to do so, and while Tinker held the torch close to the lower lock-plate, Blake detached the "spider" from the key-ring.

In appearance, the "spider" looked like some sort of strange, scaly animal, about six inches long, and no thicker than a lead pencil at one end, and scarcely more so than the lead within a pencil at the other. As it was then, it seemed straight and inflexible, but this was due to the outer covering, which consisted of dozens of very thin steel rings being pushed along the whole length of it.

At the thicker end, was a small turning ring, and when Blake had given this a few twists, the rings came back upon themselves, thus releasing, at the thinner end, four fragile-looking but finely-tempered "strands" of chrome steel. It was just there that the whole secret of Blake's invention lay.

Gently and with fingers as delicately poised as those of a surgeon in the act of performing an operation of the most delicate nature, Blake insinuated first one pair and then the other pair of "strands" into the slit of the lock-plate.

He pressed them in until perhaps half an inch had disappeared from view, and then, with the greatest care possible, he began to twist the turning-ring at the other end, first this way, then that way, all the time keeping up a gentle probing motion until he felt a very slight resistance to his pressure, at this, he paused, and removed his fingers from the turning-ring.

Now he began a sort of wiggly-waggly motion, all the time insinuating the thinner end more and more, until something more than an inch of the "strands" had disappeared within the slit.

All the time his fingers were conscious that the resistance was increasing slowly but surely, although, at that, it was still no more than would have been sufficient to break the stalk of a flower.

But Blake knew that little instrument as he knew the palm of his own hand. It was a creature of his own brain, and he knew exactly when the tiny little feelers or strands were telegraphing that they had reached the limit of twisting and probing. When that moment came, he held the "spider" in his left hand, while with his right he again took hold of the twisting ring.

This time he pressed it towards the thinner end, and click, click, click! The little rings went sliding along towards the lock-plate, until they were gripping the "strands" close to it. Blake tested the pressure carefully, then he began to turn.

At first nothing seemed to happen, except that the visible part of the "spider" seemed to be twisting round to the right. But Blake now had his ear close to the lock-plate, and when the pressure suddenly ceased, accompanied by a slight click from within, he knew that his little invention had once more proved its worth.

He had once told Tinker that it would be impossible to invent a lock which the "spider" would not conquer, and now he was beginning to believe that he was right.

From the top lock he turned his attention to the lower. The "spider" came out quite easily, and in the second instance he simply repeated the process he had employed in the first.

He worked just as delicately as before, and when at last he gave the turn to the right, he again felt the pressure slacken and a slight click within the lock. He withdrew the "spider" and slipped it into his waistcoat pocket.

Then, with a gesture to Tinker, he laid his hand on the wrought-iron handle and turned. He pressed against the panels at the same time, and the next instant the door opened as easily as if it had never known what a lock was.

Blake paused long enough to take the electric torch from Tinker. He flashed it in front of him, and found he was staring into a narrow passage, which led to a closed door some twenty feet beyond. He stepped in, and Tinker followed.

The lad shut the door softly, and together they crept along towards the closed door. They reached it safely and paused again to listen, so Blake turned the handle and pushed. They stepped into a big kitchen, looking very clean and home-like with its spotless floor and the walls lined with gleaming copper cooking utensils.

Opposite them was another door, and on opening this they found themselves in another short passage, with a door still to negotiate.

Then they stepped into the big lounge hall, which they both remembered from their first visit to the place, and, after some search, Blake found the governing switch on the inside wall of the lobby.

He gave it a press, and the next moment the whole place was flooded with light. Together they stood looking about them. Nothing seemed to have been altered since they had been there months before, and it all looked so normal that it gave one the impression that the owner must still be in residence, and might walk in upon them at any moment.

There were ashes in the big brick open fireplace, and, striding across, Blake touched them with his hand. They were quite cold, but still he was not satisfied.

He raked the ashes over until he could reach those at the very bottom. But still they gave forth not the slightest vestige of heat, so he rose.

"No sign there," he remarked, in an ordinary tone. "We shall see what the studio has to show us, Tinker. If our friend Barrow is about, he may wonder why the light should suddenly appear, but that can't be helped. We can't take the time to use only the torch."

He strode to the door which, he knew, opened to the big studio. It was not locked, and opened easily to his pressure. He entered, and felt for the switch. He gave it a tug, and then they stood gazing about them.

There were pictures everywhere. They were hanging on the wall, and leaning against it; there were scores piled in the corners, and under a great centre table; there were canvases with a mere smudge of paint on them, and some in all stages of completion, and, on a big easel, set where it would get the light at the best angle was another canvas covered with a white cloth.

Blake walked over to this and lifted the cloth. Underneath was an almost completed water-colour of a scene which it was not difficult for him to recognise as Egyptian. He dropped the cloth and swung round.

"I have a hunch that our friend is gone and has been gone for a couple of days at least. He may walk in on us but that remains to be seen. Certain things make me think though, that he expects to be away for some little time. I noticed that the inner door of the lobby was barred with a heavy strip of iron, and this studio looks as it he thought it might be a definitely long period before he would return. We shall have a look upstairs, and then I want to try and get into that big desk in the hall. It looks the most interesting bit of furniture about, but it may end in just that."

Blake switched off the light, and led the way back to the lounge, motioning for Tinker to close the door of the studio.

He crossed the hall, and started to mount the stairs, and as he did so he little dreamed that, as his foot pressed on a certain step, he started into action a particular bit of mechanism which the Black Eagle had arranged just before taking his departure.

They made a thorough tour of the top floor but found nothing there to throw any light on the problem which Blake was trying to solve.

When they had completed their tour by making a circle of the gallery above the studio, they returned to the hall, and there Blake prepared to attack the great mahogany desk which had caught his attention.

It was a very large affair, built after no particular period, but obviously designed with a view to special use by the builder.

It was, from a technical point of view a very fine piece of joinery, and, as he gazed at it, Sexton Blake recalled that the Black Eagle had learned the cabinet-making craft on Devil's Island.

"Built by himself," he muttered, "so we can take it for granted that he has forgotten nothing. Three locks to force first, my lad. Well, I think we can manage that all right, but it may be difficult to probe the secrets inside without wrecking the whole thing, and I hate to destroy a fine piece of work. However, let us see what we can do."

An examination showed that the three locks were of the same type, although of smaller size, as those on the back door. From certain faint marks, Blake came to the conclusion that they were not those which had been originally fitted, which seemed to point to the fact that the owner attached some importance to whatever he kept in the receptacle.

Under ordinary circumstances Blake would have brought his burglary kit into play, but, as he had remarked to Tinker he hated to spoil a fine piece of work, so he determined to use a little more time and make his attempt with the "spider."

His procedure was exactly the same as it had been on the locks of the back door, and slowly but surely, without marring the work in the faintest degree, he forced back first one, then another, and finally the third.

Tinker gave him a hand in pushing back the heavy roll top, and almost the first thing that met their eyes, lying just beyond the heavy blotting-pad, were two plain yellow manilla luggage labels. Blake took them up, and after a cursory glance, gave a little tongue-click of satisfaction.

"I am a little surprised at the carelessness of our absent host," he remarked, "in leaving these tags here—that is, if they do bear the same watermark as the one in our possession—then the Black Eagle has been guilty of violating one of the first tenets which he lays stress on in his own book." Blake was referring to the now famous book, "Crime and the Professional Criminal", which the Black Eagle had written shortly after his escape from French Guiana, and in which he had dogmatised in no uncertain terms regarding the mistakes made by the ordinary criminal which almost invariably led to his undoing.

He thrust the two labels in his pocket, and was again bending over the desk, when he heard a slight gasp beside him, and turning, he saw Tinker suddenly slump to the floor. He was lying in a crumpled heap, and Blake could see that the lad had been gripped by some strange seizure for his eyes were closed and his lips like chalk.

"Good heavens! What is it, my lad?" he cried in a tone of concern as he bent down.

But then he jerked up quickly, and one hand sought his throat as he staggered back against the desk coughing with the agony of the sudden suffocation which had clutched at his lungs.

He made a violent effort to recover, and as he passed his tongue across his lips he felt a strange, unpleasant salty taste. Once more he knelt, but for the second time the same strange sensation seized upon him, and forced him back, gasping and struggling for breath.

Then Sexton Blake realised that there was something very sinister at work. He knew that he must reach down and get Tinker to the open air. What had seized upon the lad he couldn't guess, and he was completely at a loss to understand why, as soon as he should attempt to bend, he should find it impossible to do so without fear of sudden suffocation.

The salty taste was still on his lips, and he felt as if something insidious was creeping into his head. His eyes were smarting, and his hands felt cold and clammy.

He brought all his will-power to bear, and for the third time struggled to get down to the unconscious lad. He plunged downward like a man tackling in football, but this time he pitched clean over the lad, striking the floor violently with his head.

Again the terrible sensation of suffocation assailed him, and his mouth seemed flooded with that nauseating salty taste. He felt his senses swimming, and he knew if he did not succeed in conquering whatever it was that was gripping him, he, too, would sink into the same unconsciousness to which Tinker had surrendered.

By a violent effort of will he struggled to his knees, and then to his feet. The moment he stood upright he felt a difference in the air, and after some moments the worst of the paroxysm seemed to pass.

Now Sexton Blake was a man who did not believe in the supernatural. Nor did he think, for a single moment that he was being affected by any sudden apoplectic seizure, which would account for such a strange seizure each time he attempted to bend down.

Even if he, at his age, should be so affected, it was ridiculous to think that Tinker would be.

He knew that something very terrible was abroad in that house just then. He knew the calibre of the man who owned it, and he knew that in some way, somehow, he had struck at them with an invisible hand while they had prowled about the premises.

Just how deadly the effect might be Blake couldn't tell, but he was in a terrible state of anxiety as he stood weakly against the desk, struggling with all his might to conquer the terrible feeling of burning and suffocation that had assailed him, and looking down at the chalky face of the lad.

He knew that in some way, human or superhuman, he must get the lad up and into the fresh air, where he could try to discover what had occurred. He cared nothing for the risk to his own life, but he knew it would do neither of them any good if he collapsed, too.

He jerked out a handkerchief and tied it about his mouth. He had an instinct that, whatever it was that had attacked them was confined to the lower level of the air, for it was only when he bent down that he felt the sensation.

Then he made another plunge towards the lad, and, although he felt the salty taste again, even through the linen handkerchief, the feeling of suffocation was not so overpowering, and he succeeded in getting his hands under the lad's shoulders.

Then he heaved upwards, lifting the lad as he did so, and clutching him in his arms, he staggered along towards the stairs.

His one idea was to reach open air. He knew that every window on the ground floor was beyond his reach, and, besides, something told him that it would be dangerous to remain there.

He stumbled up the stairs and straight along the square hall at the top. He drove in a door facing him with his foot, and crossed a small room to where he could see the dim outline of a window.

He laid the lad's unconscious form on the floor and pushed back the latch; then he lifted the sash and took one deep gulp of the fresh night air before turning back.

But even as he was on the point of doing so he saw something dark moving just beneath him. He leant forward and gazed down, realising then that the wide brick top of the side wall, which he had suspected might conceal a secret passage, was just a few feet beneath. And along this two dim figures were moving.

Blake was in a quandary. He did not know how serious Tinker's condition might be; whether the strange thing that had seized the lad and had almost conquered him as well meant death or something less.

He felt that those shadowy figures outside must have some connection with the mystery and, in any event, that they could only be there with him and Tinker as their objective.

On that thought and the sudden recollection of the anonymous letter which he had received he made up his mind. With an unspoken prayer that he was doing the right thing, he threw his leg over the sill and dropped to the brick beneath.

As he did so the two figures ahead sprang upright and began to run along the top towards the alley at the back. Blake jerked out his weapon and tore after them, but before he could overtake them he saw first one then the other disappear from view.

Two seconds later he, too, was at the end, and without the slightest hesitation he went over, stuffing his automatic back into his pocket and taking the fifteen foot drop as lightly as he could.

He landed with all muscles and joints as loose as possible, the acrobat's secret in a long drop, and as he scrambled to his feet he saw two figures just ahead of him. One of the men appeared to be limping painfully, while the other was helping him along. Blake called out a sharp command as he clawed out his automatic.

They paid no attention, their every effort seeming to be bent on reaching the public street; so Blake charged. He came up with them just before they reached the mouth of the alley, and as he threw out his hands one of the pair, the uninjured one, suddenly whirled and lunged at him. A fugitive beam of light flashed for the infinitesimal fraction of a second on cold steel, and Blake felt something slide along his shoulder.

Then he struck, using the butt of his automatic as a club. The weighted end caught the fellow full between the eyes and he went down. But in the meantime the second man had managed to drag out his gun, and the whole night seemed to shatter in one terrific explosion as the gun exploded not six inches from Blake's ear.

He was on the back swing at the time, and it was only that that saved his life. As it was, the bullet literally fanned his forehead as it ripped past, flattening itself against the brick wall.

Blake did not even have time to turn. He gave a snarl of fury and swept his left hand backwards, catching the other along the side of the head. The man fired the second time even as he staggered, but the bullet went wide, and the next moment Blake was upon him, his hand searching for the throat.

He clutched him thus, and, holding him helpless with one set of fingers, caught his right wrist in his free hand. He brought the arm up and gave it a savage twist which caused the other to release his hold of the gun, then shifting his hold, Blake deliberately hit him a terrific wallop in a half horizontal swing that landed full on the "point" of the chin. The man's head jerked back as if a pile-driver had struck him; he gave one low grunt and then lay still.

Blake scrambled up and turned to the other who was still lying just as he had fallen. He pulled out his electric torch and had just pressed the switch when he heard the sound of someone running, and a few seconds later the bulky form of a constable lumbered into the alley. Blake swung the light on him and saw that it was Barrow.

THE constable also had his lamp in action, and as he flashed it, first on the two men on the ground, then on Blake, he gave a low exclamation.

"Is it you, Mr. Blake?"

"Yes, Barrow. Put out your light for a moment. I shall do the same. I suppose some of the neighbours must have heard the sound of shots, but we don't want them here if we can help it. I will explain briefly what happened; then I think you had better 'phone through for a patrol. I shall make the charge against this pair."

Barrow did as he was bade and drew closer to Blake. The latter skimmed over his reasons for having forced a way into the house, explaining that Detective-inspector Thomas would deal with that phase of it. Then he told how, as he happened to open a window he saw two figures on the top of the wall and had gone after them.

"They dropped into the alley, and this one—he indicated the man who had been limping—must, have injured his foot or ankle. The other was helping him along when I tackled them, and I managed to knock that fellow unconscious. But this one here drew his revolver and fired twice. He almost got me the first time. That is all, except that I managed to get him down and knocked him out with a clip to the 'point.' I will remain on guard here if you will go and see about the patrol car."

"I'll go at once, Mr. Blake. Here comes someone now, Looks like a neighbour."

A man had suddenly appeared, seemingly clad in trousers, coat and an overcoat. He was bareheaded, and as he caught sight of the constable he asked what was wrong.

"Nothing much, sir," Barrow reassured him. "Just a little quarrel here. Are you the occupant of one of those houses across the road?"

"Yes—the second from the corner."

"Have you a telephone?"

"Yes. Do you wish to use it?"

"If I may."

"Then come along. Will your men be all right? What about this fellow here? He looks like an evil character."

Blake smiled at this description of himself, and the constable chuckled aloud.

"He's all right, sir," he answered. "He's one of us."

"Oh! I am sorry," was the response, but, nevertheless, Blake noticed that he still seemed a little dubious. However, he took the constable off with him, and in a few minutes Barrow was back to announce that the motor patrol was coming at once. Blake remained with him until it arrived, but when the two unconscious men had been bundled in he refused to accompany it.

"I shall go direct home," he said. "I'll bear you in mind when I make my charge, Barrow, and will see that you get full credit."

He waited just where he was until the patrol had sped off, but the moment he was again alone he lost no time in throwing the hooks of the silk ladder up to the top of the wall, for he was in a fever of anxiety to know how Tinker was faring.

He went up as silently as a shadow and, once safely on the top of the wall, pulled the ladder up after him. He turned then and, crouching low, sped along the two foot top towards the window by which he had emerged, He had no difficulty in getting back over the sill, and, as soon as he had dropped to the floor inside, he jerked out his electric torch and flashed it to the floor.

He gave a sudden gasp as he did so, for Tinker was no longer where he had left him. He swung the circle of light round the room and on to the bed, but there was not the slightest sign of the lad.

The door was partly open, and in half a dozen strides Blake reached it. There was a deep uneasiness tugging at his heart, for he felt that he should not have risked leaving the lad alone, unconscious and helpless as he had been.

He hurried along the upper square hall towards the head of the stairs, and then suddenly he paused in sheer amazement at the sight that met his eyes. About six or seven steps down was Tinker, clinging desperately to the banisters with one hand, while he clutched the right wrist of a man who held a revolver.

The lad's eyes were almost closed, and his face was still of that same deathly pallor which Blake had noticed as he lay unconscious. on the floor in the lower hall.

But the lad's will must have been driving him on for, it seemed against every physical law, that he could have held off his would-be-assassin as long as Blake now knew he must have done.

How his antagonist had got there— whether he had been in the house all the time or had entered after he, Blake, had jumped out of the window, Blake didn't know.

But as he saw the lad slowly but surely giving way beneath the savage pressure of the other, as he saw his left arm coming slowly down, Blake barked out a single, savage epithet and jumped.

He landed close beside the pair and shot out one hand, clutching Tinker's assailant by the collar. That touch was the first warning the fellow had of Blake's coming, and he gave back with a startled cry as Blake's weight bore on to him.

With a quick movement, Blake twisted his arm back and up between his shoulder-blades and, as he applied the agony-pressure of that simple ju-jitsu trick, the fellow's muscles relaxed and the pistol dropped to the step.

Blake hurled him down as if he had been a sack of bran. The fellow went crashing to the bottom, and there he flopped about like a landed fish.

Blake thought of the sensation which he, too, had experienced when he had tried to pick up Tinker, but he gave it no further thought then for the lad was sagging weakly against the banisters, and was threatening each moment to tumble after his assailant.

Blake threw his arms about him and lifted him up. He stumbled back up the stairs and on to the bedroom through which he had reached the window. He knew now that the lad must have a good chance, for it seemed that the fresh air from the open window must have revived him.

Blake laid him on the bed and spoke to him. But Tinker could only mumble a reply, so Blake dragged the bed close to the window and pushed the sash up the full way. Then he ran back through the hall to the head of the stairs and started down towards the bottom, where he could see the stranger lying crumbled up unconscious, just as Tinker had been.

But half-way down, Blake drew up with a jerk. Once again that nauseating, salty taste was in his mouth, and looking down he saw that he was a good eight feet from the floor.

He frowned and looked towards the desk where he and Tinker had been standing when the lad had dropped unconscious, then, suddenly, he gave his thigh a slap with the open palm of his hand.

"How confoundedly stupid," he muttered aloud. "How dense of me not to guess the before. I might have known the Black Eagle would not go away without leaving something deadly to guard his den."

For in a flash the truth had come to him. He raced back up the stairs and into the bedroom where Tinker lay. He took up a towel and plunged it into the water jug. This he wrung out and tied over his mouth, then he ran back through the hall and dashed down the stairs. He did not wait to see how much of the mysterious taste would percolate through the wet towel.

He was sure he had hit on the truth and, if he was right, then he knew just how much chance he had. He struck the bottom and in a swift movement caught the unconscious man under the shoulders.

The fellow was of medium size and, Blake judged, somewhere in the vicinity of eleven stone in weight. He was a hefty lump to lift to his shoulders in one heave, but Blake did it and then, breathing just as little as he could, he started back up the stairs.

At the top he paused and dumped his burden on the floor. He tore the towel from his face and dragged his burden along to the bedroom. He flung him across the bed so that his head was close to the window, and then he turned his attention again to Tinker.

The lad was trying to sit up, so Blake placed an arm behind him.

"W-what is it?" Tinker was asking, in a thick voice.

"You are all right, young 'un. It was an accident which I should have spotted before, you will be all right presently. The fresh air will revive you. I should not have left you. Can you tell me what happened?"

"I found myself lying on the floor," mumbled Tinker, "—felt rotten—couldn't see much and couldn't get up—was trying to call you when someone came through the window—thought it was you and let him pick me up—he dragged me along to the stairs and then I saw his face—saw it wasn't you and put up a fight. Couldn't do much— somehow I couldn't see—felt him dragging me down the stairs, and then saw he had a revolver—managed to get hold of his wrist—don't know any more—is everything all right, guv'nor?"

"Quite, my lad, quite. You are not to worry any more now. Just rest here in the fresh air until you feel better. If you want to know exactly what happened, you were gassed. I nabbed two birds outside, and the third was trying to 'fix' you. He is here at your feet, and as soon as he becomes conscious I am going to drag the truth out of him. We shall have to get out of here before long, for this floor will soon be flooded with the gas."

Blake rose and then made his way to the top of the stairs. He went down slowly and kept testing the air at each step with his tongue. As soon as he felt the first trace of the salty taste he drew back.

He saw that he was now standing two steps higher than when he had descended before, and from that he could gauge how quickly that invisible death was spreading.

He sought in every direction which was visible, trying to discover where the gas was coming, but he could see nothing. He backed a step and turned his head, listening. He had no intention that his prisoner should regain consciousness and again attack Tinker.

But he had not much fear of that for now, with his faculties returning, the lad should be more than a match for one who was under the influence of the same deadly gas which had handicapped him.

"I can't quite place it," Blake muttered, still studying the air beneath him. "It is perfectly invisible and yet not tasteless. It must belong to one of the heavier types of gas, for it is certainly heavier than air and only rises as it fills from beneath. That explains how it caught Tinker before I experienced anything. The lad, being shorter in height, was engulfed, as it were. It is just like an invisible sea rising slowly. It is a clever and most diabolical plan to hit on, and it is by the merest accident, that both the lad and I are not lying down there, unconscious and perhaps dead.

"How long it takes to cause death I don't know, but I am going to find out. How much there is of it I can't guess either, but we must have disturbed some secret trap which the Black Eagle left prepared and, with all windows closed, the result was almost a certainty only for the one little chance that Tinker was with me and was attacked first. You'll pay for that, my fine bird, or my name isn't Sexton Blake."

With that Blake turned and sped back up the stairs. He opened a door on the right, and switched on the light. He had remembered seeing a bottle on the washstand in one of the rooms and thought this was the one. He was right and, taking it up, he poured out the contents. He rinsed it out hastily, and then was about to light a match when suddenly he paused.

"It might be risky—the stuff may be as inflammable as coal gas—it doesn't seem that any could have been driven up here yet, but you never can tell."

He had intended creating a vacuum in the bottle by burning out the oxygen with the flame of the match, but now he took the mouth between his lips and, holding it thus, made his way back to the stairs.

He went down until he was down on the step just above that where he had been standing before, and then he sucked in the air from the bottle as hard as he could. Next he flipped the bottle out and down into the invisible gas so that the bottom was uppermost. He held it there for some time and then thrust in the cork.

Back in the room where he had found the bottle, he closed the door and got out his matches.

"I'll risk it, anyway," he thought.

He lit the match and nipped out the cork. He put his tongue to the mouth of the bottle for the fraction of a second and at once got the salty taste. Then he thrust the flame of the match into it, holding his face away in case the stuff exploded. But nothing happened except that the match went out at once.

"That's one clue," he muttered. "I'll do the rest in the laboratory."

With that he opened the door and went along to where he had left Tinker and his prisoner. Tinker was now walking up and down as if trying to clear his head, and Blake saw that his prisoner was sitting up weakly. He walked across and jerked the fellow to his feet.

He dragged him out of the room and across the hall to the head of the stairs, and there he propped him against the banister while he studied him.

He had never seen the man before, to his knowledge. But the type was familiar enough. He was of the sort to be found in the underworld in any part of London—a criminal who had probably done time several times, and would take on any "job" from petty thieving to murder for a price.

Blake shook him violently, and at last saw that the fellow was fully cognisant of what was going on.

Blake pointed downwards.

"Listen to me," he said sternly. "I don't know just what job you were trying to pull off here, or who it is that has hired you to try and murder me. But I am going to find out before I finish with you. Do you remember what happened to you when I threw you down the stairs a little while ago?"

"I dunno," mumbled the crook. "I ain't done nothin'. I saw a window open and came in. The other bird 'jumped' me and I fought. I ain't took nothin'. Let me go."

Blake dragged him down the stairs until he was close to where he figured the top of the rising sea of gas would be. There he held the man, and bending over, hissed:

"Those lies don't go with me. I know who sent you here—you and your two companions. They have been taken off in a patrol wagon, and their story is good enough for me. Your only chance is to beat them to it and get in your story first. I will tell you, in case you don't know it, that the whole hall beneath you is full of a deadly gas. That is what struck you before, and in case you don't believe it, I am going to give you another taste of it."

As he spoke he jammed the fellow's head down until it almost touched the step on which he was standing. Studying him, he saw him give a sudden gasp and then he lurched forward. At that Blake dragged him back and again propped him against the banisters.

"That is just a taste," he said, in a voice as cold as ice. "You know I am Sexton Blake all right, so there is no need for introductions. And knowing that, you will know that I always do just as I promise or threaten. Now this is what I say to you— if you don't tell me here and now under whose instructions and pay you are acting, I am going to fling you down these stairs again."

The man drew back weakly. His eyes sought Blake's, and he shuddered at the cold remorselessness of them. As a matter of fact he had known nothing about the gas which had been turned on when Blake and Tinker first mounted the stairs, but he did know that something very mysterious had attacked him when he was flung down the stairs the first time, and that second taste just then had put a horrifying fear in him.

He could have faced a bludgeon or anything he could see, but he was of the undeveloped mentality which is in deadly fear of the mysterious and unseen, and he was in a cold, whimpering sweat as he begged for mercy.

"Cut that out!" snapped Blake. "Out with the name of your employer or down you go."

Once again he jammed the other's head down until he got a further breath of the deadly gas; then he dragged him back.

"It's rising every moment," he said. "One last chance—do you speak or do I fling you down? Once you go it will make you unconscious so quickly you won't even be able to get to your feet. And it is a nasty death. Are you going to speak?"

"Don't do it, guv'nor, don't do it. I'll tell what I know."

"I'll know if you are lying, and if you try that you go down just the same."

With that, Blake forced him up to the top of the stairs, where he found Tinker standing. The lad had heard Blake's last words, but he said nothing, only watching while Blake backed his man against the wall.

"Now then," he ordered, "out with it!" Away from the imminent danger of the terror of that mysterious thing which he could not understand, some shreds of rat courage returned to the man. He shifted under Blake's grasp and looked up sideways.

"You'll let me go then, guv'nor, won't you?" he whined. "I ain't done nuthin'. I—"

But that was as far as he got. A loud crack sounded as Blake brought the open palm of his hand round with terrific force, catching the fellow on the side of the head and knocking him almost off his feet.

"Spit it out!" he snarled. "Start now or you have had your last chance."

And, realising that he had played his last card, that the grim-faced man who stood over him meant business, the old lag surrendered.

"It was Abe Manstein, guv'nor. That's all I know. He paid me and my mates to do the job. It was Manstein who had you watched and sent us after you to-night. We was to find out what you were doin' here, and spoil your game."

"You mean to do us both in if you could," returned Blake curtly. Then: "Abe Manstein! Who is he? Out with it—all of it and no more hedging. If you are making up things it will be all the worse for you."

The man looked at him in surprise, which Blake felt was genuine.

"Lumme, guv'nor, don't you know Abe Manstein? Then why has he got your number up?"

And since Blake was asking himself the very same question, he decided that the privacy of Baker Street was a better place to complete the examination than in that house of creeping death.

BEFORE attempting to leave the place, Blake took the trouble to secure another bottle of the strange gas, which he corked tightly and placed in an inner pocket. While he was doing this, Tinker kept guard over the prisoner with his automatic, and then they went out by the window which gave on to the brick top of the outer and inner false (so Blake thought) wall.

Blake it was who went first, and Tinker shepherded the prisoner along next.

The lad pulled the window down after him, for Blake had made up his mind that he would leave the gas to run itself out as it chose. He was by no means unmindful of what might happen if the supply should prove sufficient to fill the whole house, for should that be the case, and the enclosed air find difficulty in being forced out, then an explosion was almost inevitable.

But he was inclined to think the supply of gas would not be equal to this, although he had already come to the conclusion that it must be stored in a greatly compressed form somewhere in the vicinity of the lower hall, since that was where they had first felt its effects. In this he was, of course, correct.

Blake had made up his mind, too, that at the very first opportunity be would return to that house and investigate what he thought must be a secret passage along the wall.

If that theory proved right, then, he realised, it might prove a very valuable bit of information in the future, for he was beginning to believe that, no matter how long he might stay abroad at any one time, the Black Eagle's actual headquarters was the house in the crescent.

Before attempting to drop into the alley, Blake let himself down into the garden and spent nearly a quarter of an hour there, relocking the back door just as he had found it.

Then he returned to the top of the wall by means of the silk ladder, and a few minutes later he and Tinker, with their prisoner between them, were standing in the alley at the back.

Blake had no idea what had become of the constable, but he was by no means anxious to meet him for, should he do so, he could hardly avoid turning the third prisoner over to him. And he was most anxious to question the fellow further before he passed into the hands of the police.

Therefore he kept guard over the man in the alley while Tinker went off to find a taxi. In about ten minutes the lad was back, having found one in the Edgware Road, and the sharp jab of the muzzle of Blake's weapon in the prisoner's back sent him forward and into the cab without any protest.

At Baker Street the same procedure was adopted, and at last they were in the consulting-room with their man backed into one corner where Tinker could keep an eye on him while Blake turned him inside out, so to speak.

And Sexton Blake knew just how to handle a job like that. He did not use the notorious "third degree" methods so popular with American police officials, but he put on a persistent mental pressure that had his man so tangled up inside half an hour that it was not difficult to pick out what was obvious truth and discard what was obvious untruth.

And not until he was quite satisfied that he had dragged out all there was to get at did Blake stop. Then he discarded the man as one would throw out an unwanted card from a poker hand.

"Come along!" he ordered. "I haven't made up my mind what I shall do with you yet. I shall, of course, turn you over to the police; but what happens to you then will depend on what evidence I am prepared to give against you. So if you want an easy passage this time I advise you not to try to make any trouble."

They took him along to the laboratory where they bound him firmly, but did not gag him for the fellow promised he would not cry out. Then they heaved him on to a couch in one corner and left him.

They had scarcely finished when Tinker said he heard the front doorbell ringing and hurried off to see what it was at that hour of the night.

He came back shortly to tell Blake that it was Inspector Thomas who wanted to see him urgently. Blake went along at once to the consulting-room, and the moment he laid his eyes on the inspector he could see that he was in a state of considerable perturbation.

"What tricks have you been up to?" he blurted.

Before answering Blake took Tinker by the arm and pushed him into one of the low saddle-bag chairs. Then he poured out a small draught of spirit with which he mixed some soda.

"Drink that, my lad," he said gently. "You are looking pretty white yet."

"I'm all right now, guv'nor," protested Tinker; but Blake insisted, and he downed the concoction. Then Blake poured two whiskies and soda and passed one to the inspector, after which he deliberately filled and lighted his pipe. Then when he was comfortably settled in his desk chair he said, in a casual tone:

"You were saying, inspector?"

"I asked you what you had been up to to-night," repeated Thomas in a milder tone.

"I don't quite follow you. Perhaps you will explain."

"Why this business up near the Marble Arch. I was at the Yard when the arrest of two men was reported. I had the patrol come on to the Yard so I could have a look at them. And—"

"One moment, please. If you had a look at them did you recognise either or both?"

"I should say I did. Or, at least one of them who has done time again and again. We have no record that we can find of the other except that his finger prints coincide exactly with one set that Tinker left at the Yard last night. Where did you get those prints?"

"Not so fast. Did the men say what they were doing at the house near the Marble Arch?"

"They refused to talk. I understood from the patrol that it was you who would make the charge, so after watching the search for the fingerprints I came on here. What is the charge? What is that house up there? And what were you and they doing there?"

"Yes, I will make the charge," answered Blake imperturbably. "It will be one of murderous assault or, perhaps, a little stiffer than that. One of them tried his best to knife me and the other shot at me twice. I happened to be near that spot when I came upon them dropping down from the wall which bounds it at the rear. I had been there to call on the occupant, but found him not at home. Then the incident occurred."

"Is that all?" persisted the inspector suspiciously.

"What else is there to tell?" countered Blake. "They attacked me—I defended myself with Tinker's assistance—we overpowered them, and like good citizens handed them over to the police. What more could we do?"

The inspector grunted.

"That sounds all right," he muttered, "but I don't understand it just the same. What is the matter with Tinker? He looks pretty peaked."

"Tinker had a bad doing," responded Blake. "He is somewhat better now, and will be all right by the morning."

"Huh! Isn't there something else behind all this? Isn't it kind of funny that one of the men you handed over to us should have fingerprints that coincide exactly with one of the sets which Tinker left at the Yard?"

"I agree that it is a most remarkable coincidence. And I shall tell you exactly where Tinker got his set. He took them among others from a sheet of the paper which contained an anonymous letter that was pushed through our door yesterday. It was one which threatened me and me only. I set the lad to investigate it and, if it is a fact that the two sets of finger prints are identical, then I may be able, with your assistance, of course, to trace the author of the letter."

The inspector looked far from satisfied, but he could say no more. Blake had dealt with each question. promptly and, apparently, openly enough. And yet he had a feeling that there was a lot more that Blake could tell if he felt inclined.

It was Blake who broke the silence which had fallen.

"By the way, inspector, did you ever hear of a man of the name of Abe, or Abey Manstein? I have reason to believe that he is a resident of the Commercial Road, and is, ostensibly, a shipbroker."

The inspector shook his head.

"I don't seem to know the name. Why? There are a lot of birds down that way who are in the crook game up to the neck, but manage to keep, technically, just on the right side of the law."

"Well, I have a hunch that this particular bird has slipped over this time. If I am right, then there is a very good chance of caging him. Do you want to try? I do not wish to commit myself, but it is just possible that through this particular person you might gain further information of the events of to-night—such as the reason for that pair having been at the house near Marble Arch."

"Of course I want to cage him if there is a reason."

Blake glanced at the clock on the mantel.

"It is nearly two o'clock," he remarked. "If you will be at the address which I shall give you before you leave at exactly midday to-morrow or, rather, to-day, I may be able to make your visit worth while; but I can't promise anything definite."

"I'll be there. But I wish you wouldn't be so blamed mysterious about it."

Blake laughed and poured another drink.

"Here," he said, "put this under your belt, then go off and get some sleep. I have quite a lot of work to get through yet."

When he finally got rid of the inspector he made Tinker turn in and then, for the first time, he had a chance to examine the two manilla luggage labels which he had taken from the desk at the Black Eagle's house just before Tinker flopped over unconscious.

He carried them along to the laboratory and laid them on the experimenting table there. He turned on the powerful electric arc light over the table, but before setting to work walked across to his prisoner.

"I have just had a visitor," he announced pleasantly. "It was Inspector Thomas, of Scotland Yard, whose acquaintance I have no doubt you have made on many occasions. Knowing the inspector you will realise how anxious he would have been to take you along with him had he known you were here. I have said nothing—yet. I shall, of course, turn you over to the police, but it rests entirely with you whether you get a rough passage or an easy one. If I find you have lied to me—look out."

With that he walked back to the experimenting table and settled down to work. He did not bring the microscope to bear but contented himself with examining the two cards through a strong magnifying glass.

And he was not the least little bit surprised when he found that each card was identical in length, breadth and windmill watermark with the one which had been tied to the lapel of Barat's jacket.

When he had finished he laid them aside and took out the bottle of gas which he had collected at the house in the crescent.

He next arranged a triple retort, each receptacle connected with the other by a thin glass tube. He allowed the gas to filter through first one, then the next above, and so, a little into the third in such a way that he had a certain portion of the gas in each.

Then he took down three thick volumes from his laboratory library and searched about for some time until he found the section dealing with "heavier-than-air" gases.

He read for a few minutes until he struck something that held his attention closely. He studied this very carefully, turning the pages slowly as he went along and watched intently the whole time by the prisoner on the couch.

At last Blake laid the book down and drew the apparatus towards him.

"I am about to make an experiment, or several, I should say," he remarked aloud in a conversational tone. "In these three glass tubes which you see in this rack I have collected a small quantity of gas from the flood which was filling the house where I had the pleasure of meeting you and the good-luck to get my hands on you before you succeeded in murdering my assistant. I have an idea what the gas is, and if I am right then it may interest you to know that it is a most deadly one; its action is remarkably rapid on the respiratory passages, and the first sensation is one of acute and painful suffocation. But that is not its most deadly phase. One may be unconscious from it for almost half an hour, and still come round in fresh air without any very ill effects. But to remain under it a longer time than that means death, for by then it begins to turn the blood black and, I fancy, one would not look very pretty by the time death ensued."

He paused to glance at his victim who was staring at him with goggling eyes.

"I hope I am not boring you," he said casually. "Unfortunately I like, sometimes, to talk while I work, and usually do so to my assistant. It is instructive to him at the same time. But since you have been the cause of depriving me of his company to-night I must make shift with you.

"As I was saying, I am not completely conversant with this gas or, with what I suspect it is. It may be highly explosive. It may have other deadly properties which I do not suspect. I hope not for your sake. If it is explosive and an accident occurs we shall both suffer. But if it is just deadly in some other way aside from being poisonous then I am afraid you will be the only one to experience that effect, for I propose donning a mask, which will protect me."

And with that Blake, slipped on a laboratory mask and started to work in earnest while his victim writhed in terror on the couch. And, in passing, it may be stated here that that same old lag proclaimed fervently in the underworld some time later that he would rather do three years in "stir" than be cooped up alone for even one hour with "that devil Sexton Blake."

But nothing untoward happened. Blake applied test after test to the three retorts, and when he had completed his notes he checked them with the tables given in the book which he had been consulting.

They coincided almost exactly, the only discrepancies being very infinitesimal decimal quantities which could be accounted for by the natural difference in the strength of the gas which had formed the base for the standard test and that which he was employing. Then he rose, and with a pleasant good-night to his perspiring prisoner betook himself to bed.

CHAPTER 12. Sexton Blake Visits Manstein—And Forces the Truth from Him.

AT precisely eleven o'clock the next morning the Grey Panther drew up in the Commercial Road, Aldgate, exactly in front of the building which bore Abe Manstein's dirty brass plate. While Tinker stopped the engine and affixed a safety lock to the wheels, Blake beckoned to a man who was loafing along the street and put him in charge of the car.

Then they mounted the stairs to the dingy hall above. There they paused to survey their surroundings, and after a few moments Blake said:

"I think I shall tackle the door marked 'Private,' my lad. You go in through the other and see that no one leaves until I give the word. If anyone calls let him in, but not out."

"Right you are, guv'nor. I'll waggle old trusty at them if they try to get fresh." And after tapping his hip-pocket where his automatic rested the lad started for the door opposite, while Blake strode along the hall and tapped on the other.

A voice bade him enter. He turned the handle and walked in, apparently quite unconscious of any possible danger, but inwardly as wary as a cat for any trap.

He saw a little under-sized Jew seated at the single desk which the room boasted and from the description he had received he guessed it was Abe Manstein. He closed the door and began to remove his gloves.

The Jew regarded him in a puzzled way for a few moments then, suddenly, his face went the colour of putty. He jumped up, spluttering, and made as if to rush to the door leading to the other room.

If he thought his visitor would attempt to stop him he was mistaken, for Blake continued leisurely removing his gloves, a sardonic smile twisting his mouth as he watched the antics of the other.

He knew that after the first few moments Manstein had recognised him as Sexton Blake, and that told him that his prisoner at Baker Street had spoken the truth.

The Jew had jerked open the communicating door and Blake saw him bob into the next room. Then there was a terrified squeak, and he bobbed back, closing the door hurriedly after him.

Blake guessed that Tinker was well on the job and had "waggled old trusty" as he had threatened.

As Manstein sidled back towards his desk Blake smiled at him. He laid his hat and gloves and stick on the top of the desk; then he spoke.

"Is this the way you usually receive your visitors, Mr. Manstein?" he asked lightly. "You seem perturbed. What is the trouble?"

"Vat you vant?" cried the Jew, relapsing into the accent of the ghetto in his terror. "I do not vant to see you. Vat for you gom here? Go avay—go avay, or I vill call police."

Blake laughed outright. Then his face changed and his eyes hardened. Before the Jew knew what he was about Blake shot out one hand and grabbed him by the collar. He slammed him back into his chair with such force that it threatened to collapse. Every tooth in the Jew's head shook with the shock, and he sat whimpering and moaning in unintelligible Hebrew.

"Shut up!" snapped Blake. "If you don't pull yourself together and pay attention to me I'll give you something to whine about. You know whom I am—that is obvious, and your manner is confession of your guilt. Now, then, Manstein, I am going to ask you some questions, and if you don't come across with the truth, the whole truth, and nothing but the truth, then I'll treat you pretty roughly. Turn this way."

The Jew turned a chalky face towards him, but his eyes wavered and fell.

"My first question is this," went on Blake in a voice that literally throbbed with menace. "How much did the Black Eagle if you prefer it, David Stone, pay you to put a gang of assassins on my track?"

"I don't know vat you mean, mister. I don't know you—I don't vant to know you— go avay, go avay!"

Blake sighed.

"I see you must have it," he said slowly. "I was hoping I should not have to soil my hands too much on you. But it can't be helped."

Once more his arm shot out, and in one jerk he had Manstein out of the chair. Then he set to, and for a solid five minutes he gave the oily little crook one of the most finished hidings possible to conceive. He did not hurt him dangerously, but he made every blow sting severely. And he tempered each blow in such a way that the Jew thought the next would be his finish. When Blake had completed the distasteful job he threw Manstein back into the chair.

"That is just a taste," he remarked. "If I have to do it again, then you will discover what real torture is. Now will you answer my questions?"

"Vat iss it you vant to know?"

"I asked you how much money you were paid to put a gang of assassins on my track?"

"It vas not my fault. I could not refuse. I haf business mit the gentleman, and he pays vell. Vat could I do if he says: 'Abey, send out some men to vatch that man'? I ask you—vat could I do?"

"So you had much business with Mr. Stone, did you? That is interesting. Me-thinks we are getting at the meat of the matter now. Where is Mr. Stone now?"

"I don't know, mister—I don't know. He is not in England."

"Ah! That is another step ahead. When did he leave England? Now, I want the full answer to that."

"Last Saturday night. But he vill kill me for telling you!"

"You can choose which you would rather receive death from," responded Blake, with a sudden snarl. "Do you want it from me, here and now, or would you rather take your chances of dodging David Stone?"

"I vill answer—I vill answer. I am, ain't I?"—which sounded a bit complicated, but Blake understood it.

He moved closer to the desk, and tapped the Jew on the knee.

"Give me the whole story," he said curtly. "I'll know quick enough when you start to push in the lies. Come across, Manstein. I will tell you for your benefit that, at precisely mid-day, an inspector from Scotland Yard will arrive here to take you into custody. You can't escape that, no matter how you try. The inspector in question is one of the hardest nuts at the Yard, and you'll get a very rough passage if I say the word. It rests entirely with you whether the charge I shall endorse against you is one of being accessory before the fact in attempted murder, or whether I make it much milder.

"Only the truth to me here and now can save you. I am out to get track of David Stone, and I shall do so whether you talk or not. So take your choice—a certain ten years penal, or perhaps a mild eighteen months. You had to come a cropper one day, and you are lucky, I can tell you, to be able to bargain as I am giving you the opportunity to do. Now will you talk?"

And the Jew, after some reflection, decided that he would. Blake had played on his weaknesses and his fears, although he had meant every word he said, and the Jew had chosen to look out for No. 1 first.

After all, he was probably reflecting, David Stone was on his way across the Atlantic, and even if he did discover that he, Manstein—had given him away, he could cook up some plausible tale if he failed to keep clear of Stone.

So, prompted and dominated by Sexton Blake, he began to tell his story. And it says much for Blake's interest in the case on which he was at present engaged that he listened right to the end without asking a single question. Then he nodded thoughtfully.

"All right, Manstein. I think you have told me as much of the truth as it is in you to tell. I'll keep my word to you. Instead of making the graver charge against you, I shall simply endorse one of being accessory to one of attempted burglary and assault, and if you take my advice you will plead guilty. You'll get off easier by doing so. It is now just on mid-day, and if I know anything of Inspector Thomas, he should be here at any moment. So get ready to surrender gracefully."

Even as he finished speaking, Blake heard the sound of heavy footsteps in the hall outside. Then there came a tap on the door, and as it opened the healthy, red countenance of Detective-inspector Thomas came into view.

CHAPTER 13.   A Dash Across the Atlantic—Sexton Blake's Bold Plan.

JUST six days later, Sexton Blake and Tinker were in New York.

It seems a long and sudden jump from Abe Manstein's dingy office in the Commercial Road, Aldgate, to the "City of Light," but Sexton Blake had urgent and sound reasons for making the jump.

It was, of course, due almost entirely to what he forced out of the little Jew that he left London so hurriedly. It had been a tough business dragging out the truth, and even at that Blake felt there was a good deal which Manstein had kept back.

But he was convinced that he had got at the meat of it, and he knew that he could soon wreak vengeance on the Jew if he had been bluffing him, for that oily little crook was now safely caged at Brixton Prison.

Blake had been told nothing about Moses Manstein. Abe was loyal enough, or clannish enough, if you prefer, to keep his brother's name out of his tale. But he had confessed how the Black Eagle had slipped out of London on a small tramp that was bound for a French port, and how the tran-shipment was to take place in mid-Channel at midnight on the Sunday, as agreed upon with the captain of a Dutch rum-runner.

So far, so good, Blake had thought.

But he could get nothing out of Manstein as to whether the Black Eagle had been alone or accompanied by others. On that the Jew was of no use to him, and Blake did not press it too far, for he thought it quite likely that the Black Eagle would not tell Manstein more than was necessary.

Blake would have liked an opportunity to investigate further the contents of the desk at the house in the crescent, but there was no time now, and, after all, he had found exactly what he had been looking for when he laid his hands on those two blank manilla luggage labels.

It was all the proof he needed that the Black Eagle was the person with sufficient "nerve" to do what, he felt from the first, Sartel never could have done.

The point germane to the matter was that, if Manstein had told the truth, the Black Eagle should be, even then, on his way across the Atlantic. From that point Blake had worked swiftly. With his usual practice of trying to put himself in the other fellow's position, he tried to imagine just what Sartel was aiming for, and then he endeavoured to think just one jump ahead of Sartel.

Sartel—Madame Goupolis; Madame Goupolis—the Black Eagle; the Black Eagle— Sartel. Round and round he twisted the names as if he were whirling the revolving drum of a squirrel's cage, and each time and always it all came back to the same thing.

Sartel had sought the protection of the Black Eagle. Barat, in his notes to his superiors at the Surete, had stated that he had discovered that Sartel was making for some address in London.

At first it had been in Blake's mind that the Black Eagle may have been in Paris for some time, and might have been hand-in-glove with the Goupolis in the rooking of the bank through Sartel.

But now he was inclined to think otherwise. What Abe Manstein had told him had given him a new perspective of that phase of the affair.

Then there was that morning when he and Tinker had seen the Black Eagle board the London train at Parkstone Quay in Harwich, after landing from the boat just in from the Hook of Holland.

The simplest rules of deduction were sufficient to link up those incidents, and make it seem that Manstein had told the truth about the Black Eagle's visit to Rotterdam.

Lastly, that was clinched by the finding of the two luggage labels in the desk at the house in the crescent. Careless, Blake thought, on the part of the Black Eagle, and, he added, mentally, reckless to use one of those tags for the impudent message which had been tied to the lapel of Barat's coat.

But the man doesn't live who doesn't overreach himself at some time in his life, and it had been sheer chance, plus the ability of his own quick mind to seize upon trifles, that had enabled him to untangle that particular web of incidents.

So, Blake figured, if the Black Eagle was on his way to America, then it was pretty good betting that Sartel was with him. Just what arrangement he might have with Sartel was a matter for conjecture. That was what only the future could prove. Therefore, if he could reach New York in a fast liner, he had just a sporting chance to tackle his man before he was able to slip into the country via "Rum Row."

They raced up to Liverpool and managed to catch the Mauretania just two hours before she sailed. There is no faster craft afloat that the record breaker of the Atlantic, and Blake knew, if the Dutch rumrunner was to be beaten, the Mauretania could do it despite the start the other vessel had already had.

They did the crossing in under six days, and on the pier found Bryant Kennedy, one of Blake's New York agents, to meet them.

They drove at once to the Belmont in Forty-Second Street, and, over lunch, which was served at a secluded table in the big, pillared grill-room, Blake outlined the case to Kennedy.

"Of course the movements of the rumrunner will be kept as obscure as possible," he said, when he had put Kennedy in possession of most of the facts, "but it should be possible to locate her if she is hanging about just outside the twelve mile limit."

"Why, sure that won't be very difficult," agreed Kennedy. "The excise people here have got their end of the game re-organised, and they keep pretty close tabs on anything lying along Rum Row. Aside from the special patrol of armed motor-boats they are using aeroplanes now, and, if that craft is there, I can soon find out her exact whereabouts. She may or may not have a land agent here in New York. We might be able to discover that; but it will be more difficult. The majority of the rum runners these days depend mostly on peddling it over the side to those boats that can slip through the patrol and make a race of it for the shore."

"What about the highjackers?"

"They have not been so active lately, but they are still knocking about. You never can tell when they will break out."

It should be explained here what Blake meant when he referred to the highjackers. Along with all the bootlegging lawlessness that has grown up in the United States since the advent of prohibition, there has developed a class of sea pirate who is quite as ruthless and daring as any buccaneer who ever roamed the Spanish Main in the days of Morgan and Kidd. His particular prey is the rum runner lying off the twelve mile limit and that individual, being himself on illegal business bent, has no recourse to the law. It is simply a case of "dog eat dog," and the devil take the hindmost. There have been some hot fights pulled off along Rum Row during the past few months, and, in more instances than one, when the highjackers or pirates have got the better of it they have not stopped at scuttling the ship, after emptying her of her valuable cargo of spirits, crew and all. Or perhaps they will strip her clean and then turn her loose at sea. Many lives have been lost and many more will be lost, and the bootlegger ashore doesn't care two straws how the business goes for which ever wins, highjacker or rum runner, he is sure of getting his supplies. As for the revenue cutters, they simply stand off and let the fight run its course. The more rum runners and highjackers who are killed by each other reduces the number with which they have to contend by just so many; and, after all, the devil usually manages to collect his own in the end. Hence Blake's question about the highjackers.

"What is the name of this Dutch craft?" asked Kennedy, after a pause.

"The 'Van Boten.' I looked her up in Lloyd's list before leaving London, and find that she is privately owned—the commander being the principal shareholder. His name is Gemeaker. "

"Um. Well I have a friend in the revenue department. As a matter of fact the new organisation of the revenue patrol along Rum Row is mostly due to him. I can easily put a request through to him to find out if this craft is out there. We ought to be able to hear in a few hours—even this afternoon, for he is in wireless touch with all his boats out there."

"Good fellow! I wish you would."

"I shall do so immediately after lunch. What plans have you made—if any?"

"None—yet. That is why I asked you about the highjackers. You see, Kennedy, my idea is that my man will try and get ashore as soon as he can. I have been trying to figure out just what his idea is, and I have come to the conclusion that he will try one of three things. I think he will plant Sartel here in America somewhere and let him shift for himself; or he may try to reach Mexico; or, again, he may be headed for some place across the Pacific. I don't know what his arrangement with Sartel is, but I believe, for some reason or other, he is helping Sartel to make a run to cover.

"If I am right then the Black Eagle will try to slip ashore by one of the first bootlegging boats that goes out to Rum Row. It would be as easy for them to run through a human cargo as cases of spirits. And once ashore here in New York he could soon disappear along any one of a dozen underground routes of which we both know."

"You said a whole mouthful, then, Blake. That is just what any fugitive is likely to do."

"Well, we can't utilise the revenue boats beyond the twelve mile limit. We might arrange to have them keep a watch, and if they are well on the alert they might make the capture while our man is being run ashore. But I am afraid he might slip through the net. I don't want to take any chances. There is nothing definite against the Black Eagle in this affair other than his complicity in the killing of Barat—if he did that job—and his assisting a fugitive to escape.

"But there are very definite charges against Sartel, and I have a particular reason for wanting to lay my hands on him. I have pledged my word to the prefect of police in Paris that I shall catch the man who killed the two Surete men in Brittany if it is humanly possible."

"Well, you know I shall do everything in my power to help you. I don't think you would be wise to ignore the revenue boats altogether. They might be of quite a lot of use to you. But putting that aside what other plan have you in mind?"

"I shall, of course, be only too grateful for any assistance the revenue boats can give me. But I think we stand a better chance by direct action. That would only be possible if we could arrange in some way to get right among the craft along the row."

"Just how do you mean? All I can think of is that we might, by a bit of delicate work, get one of the bootleg boats to run us out."

Blake shook his head.

"That wouldn't do. I have thought of that already. We should have to fix up something that would get us right on to the craft we want, and in such a position that we could pick our man off if we got the chance of our getting in with any of the highjackers. I don't suggest, for a single moment, that we should start any piracy or bloodshed. Heaven forbid!

"But if any of these gentry are about to make a raid on Rum Row then it would facilitate matters for us if we could take a hand in it, providing the Van Boten should happen to be one of the ships to be raided. Of course, I realise we should have to pay well, but we could do that. There is a pretty big reward out for Sartel, and the French authorities have given me practically carte blanche in the way of expenses."

"Huh! You have suggested something I had not thought of. It is a bold idea of yours, but I see the advantage of it if it could be worked. It would be a big risk and might have a very different ending from what you may anticipate. Still, all those birds are reachable—if there is such a word —if there is enough money in sight. The big problem would be to get in touch with one of them,"

"That would have to be your job, Kennedy, And from what I

know of you in the past I fancy you could reach that particular section of the underworld if you set your wits to it."

Kennedy grinned boyishly.

"I could do that all right; but the question is could I do any good by it. At any rate I could try—if you let me use my own methods."

"Most assuredly. I'll foot the bill for whatever amount you suggest. But time is the chief essence of the matter. I think we can take it for granted that our man— or men—will try to run the blockade of the revenue men just the very first chance they get. The longer they stick out on Rum Row the less chance they have of getting through."

"I'll tell you what I will do. I shall go off at once and see my friend in the excise department. Then I'll pull a couple of strings of which I know, and see if I can get in touch with one of the highjacker gangs. They are running as wide open as the Hudson over in Hoboken, and I know a few tough birds over there that might fall for it. Anyway, you can depend on me to do my best. If you have nothing of any importance to attend to, I think either you or Tinker should stick close to the hotel until I show up in case I send you a message through."

"Certainly. That is our only business in New York this time, and we shall be right here when you 'phone, or send, or come."

CHAPTER 14. Kennedy's Plans—The Attack on Rum Row—Conclusion.

BRYANT KENNEDY neither telephoned nor sent a messenger. He came in person and in a state of great excitement; at least, Blake could see it, although he was outwardly as collected as always. But up in Blake's private sitting-room he let himself go freely.

"I've fixed it," he announced, slapping Blake and Tinker simultaneously on the shoulder. "If it weren't that I was turning highjacker to-night I could put the Excise people wise to a nice little coup. So get into your glad rags—which, in this case, means the oldest duds you have—and 'yo ho for a bottle of rum!'"

Blake and Tinker laughed; then Blake asked:

"What have you arranged, Kennedy?"

"To-night we turn pirates—Morgan, and Kidd, and Bully Hayes, and Blood, and the whole caboodle wrapped up together. I went over to Hoboken after I left you. I tapped several places over there, and at last I ran into the very man I wanted to see. That bird would have been in Sing Sing now if it hadn't been for me, and he is duly grateful.

"Well, to make a long story short, I sounded him; but he was as tight as a drum. But I knew he was mixed up with both bootleggers and highjackers—he is one of those guys that take a hand either way, just as it pays best—and I persisted. Then I showed him the colour of my money, and he began to show a little interest. But I had to come across with the true reason before I succeeded in getting past his defences. He knew I wouldn't lie to him, and when I gave him my solemn word that I shouldn't breathe a whisper to the Excise, or take any advantage of what he told me, he unloosened.

"As I told you, the highjackers have been lying low for some time. He told me it was because they wanted to get full knowledge of the new revenue patrol. But they have been planning a big raid on Rum Row, and I'll say we are in luck, for to-night is the night fixed on."

"You couldn't have brought better news, Kennedy. And it is a certainty that we go?"

"A stone-cold cert. So get changed as quickly as you can. If you want any old things I can lend them to you. I must go and get into something, too, and I'll come back for you inside an hour. We have to motor out to a certain spot on Long Island to the rendezvous. I'll take

my car, and we can drive it right on to the ferry."

"Splendid! I think we have enough with us in the shape of old things that will do for the adventure. So you go along, and we shall be waiting for you. I think you had better pull your car in at the Murray Hill entrance, it will be less conspicuous than the other."

Kennedy nodded, and took himself off. As soon as he was gone Blake and Tinker set to work to dig out the oldest garments they had brought with them, and as they had thought to pack some loose things for gymnasium work on board the Mauretania, they soon had an outfit that was not unlike the one they had worn that eventful night at the Black Eagle's house in London.

They sat then until the hall porter on the Murray Hill side of the hotel telephoned up to say that Kennedy was waiting.

They descended at once, calm outwardly, but inwardly highly amused at the suspicious glances cast at them by the liftman. He had never seen anyone quite so disreputable-looking in the exclusive Belmont before, and they laughed outright when they saw a bulky man who had been tipped off by the liftman to follow them to the door.

As a matter of fact, he was just on the point of questioning them when he spotted Kennedy talking to the doorman, and then the truth dawned on him. He retired with a sheepish grin, and Blake and Tinker followed Kennedy across the pavement to the latter's long, low racing car, in which they had ridden many a time before.

Then they started, and inside a quarter of an hour Kennedy was guiding the car into one of the Long Island ferries.

It was a sixteen-mile run down through some of the quieter parts of Long Island to their rendezvous, and still daylight when they reached a tiny secluded cove, where they saw a long, powerful-looking motorboat drawn up at the beach.

On their appearance more than a score of men suddenly appeared from the concealment of some bushes near at hand, and they found themselves covered with revolvers from every possible angle.

They put their hands up without the slightest delay. Blake and Tinker left it to Kennedy to do the talking, for they had rarely gazed upon a tougher-looking mob of roughnecks than the bunch in front of them.

They knew, too, that it is the custom of the bootlegger and the highjacker to shoot first and ask questions afterwards.

But Kennedy apparently had spotted the man with whom he had made the arrangements, for he called out the name "Joe," and one of the most villainous-looking of the whole gang rolled forward. He nodded to Kennedy, and then gave Blake and Tinker a close scrutiny.

"So you're Sexton Blake, the big noise in the 'bull' line over in little old England?" he asked roughly.

Blake held his eye steadily.

"I am flattered to think you have heard of me," he said coolly.

The highjacker grunted, and examined Tinker. Then he turned back to Kennedy.

"I've told these other guys what you want. They ain't got no objection if yu pays right, and don't split the wind to the bulls. Do yu get me?"

"Sure I get you!" responded Kennedy cheerfully. "I have already passed my word that none of us will split a single thing. You know me well enough to know that no matter how much I may go after you guys when it is my business to close, I am no snitcher and no stool pigeon. You can take my word, and I also vouch to the limit for my friends."

"I guess you're on the level, bo'," conceded the highjacker. "And if yu ain't, yu had better order a tombstone. But these guys want tu see the colour of your money first."

"How much for the job?"

"There's twenty-five of us altogether. We want a hundred bucks apiece."

Kennedy looked at Blake.

"Two thousand five hundred dollars, Blake—five hundred pounds. That's a pretty stiff figure. Can you go that high?"

"If we must, then we must," responded Blake.

As he spoke he thrust his hand inside his waistcoat and pulled out a thick wallet. At sight of this the ring of revolvers was lowered, and the whole bunch moved forward. Blake opened it, and with a steady hand took out a wad of "greenbacks" (American currency) that, to use Tinker's expression, would choke a horse. He held this in his hand and glanced slowly round the circle, finally his gaze came to rest on Joe.

"I've got exactly three thousand dollars here," he announced pleasantly. "You have stated two thousand five hundred as your price, and I accept that. I also wish to say, here and now, that under no circumstances whatsoever will I or my young assistant breathe the slightest word of what may happen this evening. And Mr. Kennedy will tell you that I keep my word. And, moreover, just to remove any temptation you may have to knock me on the head for the other five hundred, I will say that if you land me on the deck of the ship which is my objective I shall throw in the other five hundred for good measure. Does that go?"

"You talk like a sportsman and a gentleman, boss," said the highjacker. "You can depend on us. Just pass over the dinero and we'll get going."

Blake counted off twenty-five hundred-dollar notes and handed them over. The other five he stuffed back in his wallet. Then Joe showed Kennedy where he could drive his car in under the trees where it would be safe until their return, after which all hands piled into the motor-boat, and, with the exception of Joe and two others, down into the cover of the cabin, so that any passing Excise patrol might not get too inquisitive.

Night fell while they were chugging along out to sea, and it seemed to Blake and Tinker that they must be going some distance past the twelve-mile limit, for, although they were travelling at a pretty good clip, they were still forging ahead at the end of half an hour.

They had passed one dangerous-looking craft on the way, but it had not hailed them. If it were one of the excise patrols, those on board were probably content to wait until the other should try to run back in with a cargo on board before attacking.

As a matter of fact, the highjackers' boat did not slow down until they were a good twenty miles from the shore. Then she stopped, and a hail from the cockpit brought those in the cabin out on the run.

Not a biscuit-throw away was a small, dirty-looking tramp steamer, riding easily on the long, glassy swell of the still night. The highjackers had certainly been lucky in their choice of a night for the raid on Rum Row.

In a few moments they were alongside, and one after the other they went up over the side. Apparently the little arrangement made with Kennedy was to be retained as a secret by Joe's bunch, for nothing was said about the three extra men who were accepted at ordinary hands.

One man was left in the motor-boat to stand by at that spot for their return, and then they steamed slowly southwards until away over the water a single rocket flared into the sky and burst into a thousand stars.

At that the little tramp increased her speed, and as they went along they saw first one and then another vessel loom up out of the night. Blake was standing close to Joe, and asked him how many ships would be taking part in the attack.

"Seven if they all turn up," he answered.

"And, believe me, we'll need them. There are thirty-six vessels along Rum Row now, and nearly every one has a special armed guard on board. But we'll get our meat all right. Your ship—the Van something —is seventh down the line, so our spy reported this afternoon. The excise guys may have their aeroplanes to scout along the Row, but we have one of our own, and our information gets to us just as quick as theirs does. When we board, then you can shove that other five hundred across to me, for you will probably get knocked on the head, and I ain't no wet nurse."

Blake laughed softly. He thrust his hand in his pocket and again drew out the wallet.

"Here," he said, "better take it now. I believe you are on the level and will see that I reach the deck of that vessel if it is possible."

Joe did not refuse the money, but he shot a glance at Blake that held a new respect in it and although Blake did not know it, the highjacker was vowing to himself that this darned Britisher was sure a square guy, and he'd see to it that he did get on to the deck of the Dutch rum runner."

But there was no time for further conversation then, for another rocket shot into the air, and then the night seemed to break into a perfect medley of shouts and curses and the rattle of blocks and metal and whatnot—some seemingly close at hand, others farther away, and still more just faint belated echoes reaching them over the water.

On top of that they appeared to plunge right into a dark line of mysterious-looking ships where not a single light was showing. And Blake and Tinker knew that at last they were in the very midst of the notorious anchorage of modern spirit smugglers known as Rum Row.

They will talk about that fight on Rum Row for a good many years to come. Joe had named the number of anchored craft correctly when he had said thirty-six.

There was every sort of craft there conceivable except, perhaps, a

Chinese junk. There were little low blue nose schooners from up Nova Scotia and Newfoundland way; there were reckless trawlers from half a dozen ports in England and France; there were dirty old steam tubs and others that looked more like battered tin kettles than anything else.

There were barques and one full-rigged ship; there was a beautiful white yacht that had an English baronet on board. There were little schooner craft up from the West Indies, and even a dhow-fashioned craft from the Mediterranean.

And each and every one was there for the sole and only purpose of getting liquor past the twelve-mile limit into the country where several millions of thirsty citizens of the land of the free were waiting to pay any fantastic price the bootleggers might demand. It was a priceless sight in this year of grace nineteen hundred and twenty-five.

And storming down upon the fleet like so many vicious hornets were the battered and grotesque vessels of the highjackers. They attempted some sort of regular formation, and at the third signal of the rocket each craft picked its foe and crashed in.

Never did the old pirates of the Spanish Main board a Spanish galleon running home with a cargo of ingots of gold or silver, or headed outward to New Spain with her holds full of precious silks and chests of doubloons and pieces of eight, go over the side more fiercely than did those hordes of highjacker roughnecks dash into the fray that night.

Sexton Blake had been in a good many queer situations, but he had never seen anything quite like that. It was as if all the famous buccaneers of old had suddenly torn loose in a modern setting.

With the difference that there were no heavy guns, it was something like a miniature naval engagement between two Central American republics, with a wildness and ferocity added that they couldn't have summoned in a hundred years.

Every known type of small weapon was being employed, from small, handy automatics to rifles and shotguns, marlinspikes and crowbars, rusty old cutlasses, and, on the craft from the Mediterranean, ancient curved Arab swords.

For three-quarters of a mile along Rum Row the pandemonium was terrific, and the newest of the Excise patrol boats must have thought the whole bunch of rum runners had suddenly gone berserk from their own illegal cargo.

How they ever crashed into the Van Boten neither Blake nor Tinker ever could have told. But in they did go, and almost before they knew the signal had been given they were over the side, shouting and yelling and into the thick of it with the others.

If they thought it was going to be a walkover they were rapidly undeceived, for no sooner had the grappling-irons been clinched than they were greeted with a heavy volley from the waist of the tramp.

Some of the highjackers went down; but the vicious defence seemed only to increase the savagery of the other roughnecks, and as they poured on to the deck they went into the fray with screaming curses, and, from one shrill, profane mouth, the cry of no quarter.

What followed beggars description. Somewhere a single riding-light had sprung into being, and by this ghostly flame it was as if a horde of fiends from the Pits of Darkness had suddenly appeared on the face of the sea.

Blake, keen only to discover the Black Eagle and Sartel, drew to one side with Tinker and Kennedy close to him. For them was no part of this murderous butchery. Duty had made them take advantage of what they could not prevent, but not until a hand was lifted to strike them down could one of them shoot.

And Joe and his fellows had long ago forgotten them. The whole deck seemed to reek with the smell of spirits. More than the smoke of battle had it penetrated the nostrils of the highjackers and excited them to a fury of desire.

And if it had driven them stark with unholy longing, it had incensed the defenders to equal fury in their determination that they should not lose it.

Every evil passion which has ever defiled man was let loose on that deck as the three watched; and not one good one dared lift its head, even for a moment, in that carnage of madness.

The highjackers, right in the face of volley after volley, had driven the defenders along the waist towards the poop, and to Blake it looked as if they were getting the better of it slightly.

But the crew rallied, and came back with a rush, and it was then, as he passed under the glare of the riding-light that Blake saw the man he had come so far to find.

The Black Eagle was in the very thick of the fight, and even as Blake watched he saw him shoot out his powerful hands and grip one of the highjackers by the throat.

Blake shot out a word to Kennedy and Tinker and rushed forward, fighting savagely to reach his man. Somehow he managed to get through the press, and then not more than a dozen feet separated the two enemies.

Blake raised his voice to its highest pitch and called. The cry must have reached the Black Eagle, for he turned and stared through the gloom. Blake tore off his cap and jammed ahead still more until the beams of the riding-light fell on him.

He saw a look of slow wonder appear on the Black Eagle's countenance; then he was pushed back out of sight as the highjackers made a fresh rush and drove the crew back again to the poop. Blake, Kennedy and Tinker followed, and in some way Blake managed to work his way to the short steps leading up to the poop.

He was standing there when he again caught sight of the Black Eagle. He was near the companionway by the binnacle and two others were standing beside him. Blake thought he could recognise the squat, ugly form of the Black Eagle's hunchback brother, but the other member of the trio was a mere blur. He thought it might be Sartel.

He fought like a demon to reach the poop, and at last he made it. Half a dozen highjackers got between him and the Black Eagle, but he dragged up Kennedy and Tinker and then drove a way through.

Two highjackers jumped in ahead of him, and he saw one of them begin to shoot with a heavy automatic. The lead spread in a perfect hail about the trio near the stern, and Blake saw one of them crash to the deck.

Blake kicked and struggled to drive a way to his objective, and at last he was clear of the press. Kennedy and Tinker were covering him from behind, but by that time the Black Eagle and his brother had disappeared, though, even above the fury of the melee, Blake was certain he heard a loud, mocking laugh sweep along from somewhere aft.

He tore round the corner of the companion, and was just in time to see two figures silhouetted against the sky.

The next moment they disappeared, taking the water in a clean dive, and even as he rushed towards the rail the full fury of the fight surged over and engulfed him as the crew were driven back in a last stand.

Ten minutes more and it was all over. The highjackers had won, but at a terrible cost. They drove the remnants of the crew forward and locked them in the fo'c'sle; then they laid to to get as much of the cargo transferred before morning as possible.

Down the line of Rum Row the fighting was still going on here and there, but it was fast dying down. Some of the smugglers had managed to slip their cables and make a run for it, but the greater majority fell under the combined assault of the highjackers, and, while no official figures ever were available, it was said on an authority that might be accepted as pretty close to the mark, that the battle claimed forty-nine men dead among both smugglers and highjackers; two craft sunk at anchor; one hundred and sixteen men wounded more or less seriously; and thirty-five thousand cases of liquor captured by the highjackers.

It was a bigger loot in value than Drake got when he sacked Portobello, at that time the richest city along the Spanish Main.

It was not until the highjackers were busy transferring the cargo that Blake and Tinker and Kennedy were able to search for the man Blake had seen shot down. At last they found him among a heap of wounded, and between them they carried him down to the saloon, where they saw another man sprawled out on the floor, dead.

A very brief examination of his papers revealed that he was the captain of the smuggler, who had, apparently, fallen down the companion after being mortally wounded.

Then they bent over the man they had carried down, and, as Blake saw that he lived, he signed to Kennedy to hand him a bottle of brandy which was in the rack. He forced some of the spirit between the man's lips, and after a little his eyes opened.

He gazed up vaguely, and Blake saw that it was out of the question that he could live long. He addressed him in French.

"Sartel," he said gently, "Sartel—do you hear me?"

The man moved his lips, and, bending close, Blake heard him whisper:

"Oui!"

"You can't last long, Sartel," he went on, for he knew that it would be a mistake not to tell the man the truth. "You are mortally wounded; but if you will tell me the truth, I shall carry out any last wish you may make."

"Who—are—you?" whispered the stricken man, with an effort.

"I am Sexton Blake—a detective from London. I know all about your case. I followed you and the Black Eagle from England. He has deserted you—he and his brother. They dived into the sea. They may drown, or they may reach the shore or some other vessel. But you, Sartel, are past human aid. It will be better if you do what you can before you die to clear things up. Will you answer my questions?"

"He said he would leave me if things went wrong," whispered Sartel. "But he didn't get the money. I told him I would hand it all to him when we landed. It is under the mattress in my cabin."

"All right. I'll find it. Now will you answer my questions?"

The man's eyes closed, and his head fell back. Blake thought he was gone, but he gave him some more brandy, and after a little Sartel whispered:

"What do you want to know?"

"Did you kill the two men of the Surete in Brittany?"

"Yes—they know, that."

"Who killed Barat?"

"I—did."

"But you did not tie that label to his coat and dump him off in front of Scotland Yard?"

"No—it was Stone."

"What had he to do with the embezzlement in Paris?"

"Nothing."

"It was only you and Madame Goupolis?"

"Yes."

"Then why did you seek out Stone?"

"She—gave—me—his—address.—If—you —want—to carry— out—my dying—wish— find—that—woman—and—avenge—me.— I—"

But there his voice failed him; again his head fell back, and this time his troubled spirit winged its way from that scene of evil and slaughter into the immaculate ether of the starlit cosmos above.

Blake laid him back gently and rose.

"Poor wretch!" he said softly. "He has paid a terrible price for his weaknesses and mistakes. But let us try and find his cabin and get possession of the money belonging to the French bank before any of the highjackers find their way down here. Once they smell that out we shall never touch it."

*   *   *   *   *   *

There is little more to tell. It was not until the first faint streaks of dawn were rimming the east that Kennedy and Blake and Tinker could make any attempt to get away. By this time the highjackers had broached several cases of whisky, and, to the three detectives, it was obvious that it would be hopeless to depend on Joe and his companions to put them ashore.

They held a consultation, and decided on a bold expedient. This was nothing less than the stealing of one of the ship's boats and making a dash in through the twelve-mile limit.

So they searched swiftly until beneath the mattress on one of the bunks they found a thick paper packet which Blake put in his pocket.

But it was not until the next day that he found it contained no less than the equivalent of four million three hundred and fifty thousand francs—or almost half of the total defalcations of the absconding Sartel.

They got away without being seen, or, if they were, without being challenged, and ten minutes later were surrendering to one of the Excise patrols. It was a good thing for them that Kennedy had a private letter from his friend in the department, otherwise it might have gone hard with them.

But a smaller patrol was signalled, and just as the sun was rising they bobbed in under the Battery Pier.

One person was a good deal disgruntled when, on his return to England, Blake gave him the details of the case. That was Detective-inspector Thomas, of Scotland Yard, but, after all, he had his consolation in the realisation that the impudent slap at the Yard had been well avenged in the routing of the man who had done it, and the murder of Barat in the death of the weak and foolish Sartel.

Needless to say, Monsieur Dupuis, the prefect in Paris, was deeply grateful to Sexton Blake for the swiftness with which he had brought the absconding banker to book, but the most tangible expression of gratitude came from the bank which Sartel had all but wrecked.

It had been rumoured that, owing to his large defalcations, the bank would be forced to suspend payment, but, owing to assistance from one of the other big Paris banks, and the timely arrival of Sexton Blake with nearly half the sum which Sartel had got away with, the situation was saved, and thousands of depositors paid in full.

But the most pleased person in the whole business was Tinker, for he never tired of reminding Blake that it was all due to his remark at lunch that Blake had first got a hunch that the Black Eagle might be mixed up in the business.

As for the man whom Blake had kept prisoner in the laboratory and had handed over to the police before leaving for New York as well as Abe Manstein and the other two who were captured at the house in the crescent, they all received sentences, though Abey, as Blake had promised, got off with only eighteen months. Which, considering the many rascalities the Jew had been mixed up in in the past, was much lighter than he had any right to expect.

But naturally Manstein did not look at it in that light.

Of the Black Eagle and his brother nothing was heard, but Sexton Blake did not doubt that, in the future that strange, morose criminal would again show his hand.

The End.
[48000 words]

DICK MARSTON'S PERIL.
A RATTLING, COMPLETE ADVENTURE YARN.
Author Unknown.

CHAPTER 1.   An Awkward Predicament.

THE "rag" had fallen, and the odd mixture of Europeans, half-breeds, and negroes, who patronised El Teatro del Esmeralda, the wooden structure which was the headquarters of dramatic art in Cabellano, was rapidly emptying.

"I say, Clinton," remarked Dick Marston to his chum, the gentleman who was billed as the "World-renowned Clog-dancer"—"did you notice those two fellows in uniform—some swell officers, I reckon— who were in the front seats—stalls, I suppose they are; but the deuce only knows what they call them here?"

"Can't say I did," replied Barry Clinton, as he removed the make-up from his face in a rough-and-ready way, by means of vaseline and a rough towel. "But what about them?"

"Oh, nothing! Only when I came on in my last act, they stared as though their eyes were coming out of their heads."

"Take it, dear boy, that you've 'struck ile,' as they say further north. We shall see you being commanded to appear before the king, queen, or whoever rules this infernal place before long. But there! Tata! I'm off!"

Not many minutes after the above recorded conversation, Marston emerged from the stage door, and paused to light a well-seasoned briar before making his way to the ohacara, or boarding-house, where he lodged.

It was a perfect night, such as one rarely sees, except in that portion of the globe. A moon like molten silver brilliantly illuminated one side of the narrow road, causing the other, by contrast, to be wrapped in ebony darkness.

Slowly he strolled along the almost deserted streets, drinking in the cool evening breeze, so refreshing after the heat of the day, when he suddenly became aware that another pedestrian some little distance in front, was making his way in the same direction as himself.

Without exactly knowing why, Marston followed the unknown with his eyes, till suddenly, to his intense surprise, he saw the man spring into the roadway, as a shrill cry echoed across the narrow thoroughfare, and at the same instant the actor became aware that three other forms darted from the shade, and before he could fully realise what had happened, the men were struggling together with the ferocity of wild animals.

"Three to one! Hang it all, I can't stand by and see that!" muttered Dick Marston; and, without waiting to consider the consequences, he dashed to the rescue of the unknown.

A couple of strides only separated him from the combatants, when an arm was raised aloft. The glint of moonlight fell upon cold steel; but the blow never descended, for, seizing the wrist that held the knife, Marston wrenched it back, causing the owner to release his hold.

Even as he did so, he was conscious that he was seized from behind, and in less time than it takes to relate, found himself engaged in a fierce struggle with the mysterious assailants.

It was just as well for the Britisher that he had served a rough apprenticeship in his early days, and was well acquainted with the use of the weapons with which Nature had endowed him, for a stinging blow between the eyes caused one of his foes to measure his length upon the ground, whilst a smart upper-cut sent a second man reeling backwards.

In the meantime, the stranger on whose behalf he had interfered, having risen to his feet, laid about him with a stick that he carried to such effect that the would-be assassins were beaten off, and, evidently thinking discretion the better part of valour, took to their heels.

Panting from his violent exertions, Dick Marston faced round upon the rescued man.

"Why, hang me!" he exclaimed, when he had sufficiently recovered his breath— "hang me, if it isn't Pedro!" recognising, as he spoke, the swarthy features of the leader of the small orchestra employed at the theatre.

"Si, senor," replied the man. "'Tis I. You have saved my life, and I am for ever grateful. But stay not here. 'Tis not safe, even now!"

After his recent experiences, Marston fully realised the soundness of the advice, and side by side the two men hurried from the scene of the encounter, nor did they pause till they had reached a well-lighted main street, in which they were safe from a sudden attack.

During the brief walk the Britisher had naturally tried to elicit some information from his companion as to the cause of the murderous assault upon him, but the Spaniard was reticent.

"All, senor," he said, "there are things 'tis best not to talk about. Question me, I pray, no further. You are brave, and, but for you, I should now be dead. Remember one thing. You are in a strange place amongst strange people. As you value you life, mention not what you have seen to-night. Forget it, as though it were a dream, but rest assured that Pedro will ever remember you. Buenos noches (Goodnight)!" And, without another word, he darted across the road, and was lost to view.

* *　　*　　*　　*

The following evening, as Dick Marston came down to the footlights, the first thing his eyes rested upon were the two officers who had attracted his attention the previous night, and again they seemed to criticise him keenly.

"Wonder what the deuce they are up to?" he thought to himself, as he went through his business, and when his turn was over and he left the stage clear for the Sisters Clarebell in their skipping-rope act, he noticed that they immediately vacated their seats.

"Dick, old man," laughed Barry Clinton, as they met in the tumble-down structure that did service for a dressing-room, "your friends were in the front again, I see, to-night."

"Yes; so I saw. Wonder what on earth attracts them?"

"Not your face, evidently, sonny," laughed his chum. "Hallo, what's up?"— as the negro who guarded the portals reserved for the artists suddenly appeared. "What's up, Sambo?"

"Card for Massa Marston," replied the black, grinning broadly; and he held it out as he spoke.

Dick took the proffered piece of pasteboard, and gave vent to a low whistle as he glanced at it.

"Listen to this, Barry," he said, and he rapidly read: "'General le Condo do Llomurcia requests the pleasure of Senor Marston's company at supper. A carriage is at the theatre to await his service.' What do you make of that, Barry?"

"Don't know," replied his companion sagely. "Any address?"

"Yes. 15, Calle de la Paz."

"That's the swagger street facing the cathedral!"

"Yes."

"Well, what do you intend to do?"

"Do? Why, go, of course! You'll see it in all the local papers to-morrow. Senor Dick Marston was a distinguished guest at the house of General de What's-his-name. You know the usual style. Jove! After this I'll have to make old Deeler put my name on the bills in three-inch type!"

"Well, old man, I wish you luck," replied his chum.

"Thanks! I only wish you were coming, too. But such is life!" And, with a laugh, Marston sprang down the rickety stairs, and, entering the carriage he found waiting, was swiftly driven away.

CHAPTER 2.   Where Death Hovers Nigh.

"YOU refuse?"

"Most certainly I do!" emphatically replied Dick Marston.

"Sacramento! You British were always fools!" replied the first speaker, shrugging his shoulders. "You are offered two hundred milreis gold for a trifling service, and you decline them. Well, since you will not accept payment, we must try other means." And General de Llomurcia raised his hand.

Instantly Marston felt himself seized in an iron-like grip; a rope was passed over his shoulders and firmly secured to the chair upon which he was seated, and before he could recover from his surprise, the muzzle of a heavy army revolver was pressed against his temple.

It will be necessary here to explain how the actor came to be in the precarious position in which we find him, and, to be as brief as possible, it simply amounted to this. Upon entering the carriage that awaited him at the theatre, he had been swiftly conveyed to the palatial residence in the Calle de la Paz, where he was received, as he half expected, by one of the officers he had noticed at the theatre, who introduced himself as General le Conde de Llomurcia.

"Pleased to meet you, Senor Marston," he said, cordially shaking hands. "I particularly desired a few words of private conversation, hence I requested the pleasure of your company at supper to-night. But come! It is ill to talk fasting. We will have supper first, and discuss business afterwards." And, without further comment, he led his guest into a brilliantly-lighted salon, where half a dozen other officers were already assembled.

The meal that followed was perfect in every way. Generous wines were in abundance, and instead of being in a small South American Republic, Marston could almost imagine that he was at the Ritz or Delamonico's; and as his host—who spoke English well—made himself most agreeable, the Britisher gave himself up to the pleasures of the hour, whilst inwardly wondering what could be the outcome of it all.

In due time the cloth was cleared, and the negro servants having retired, General de Llomurcia drew his chair close, and laid before the astonished actor a proposition so astounding that he had some difficulty in persuading himself that he was not dreaming, and that the brilliant scene before him would not at any moment fade away.

"Senor Marston," said the general, "you are doubtless burning with curiosity to learn the private matter I have to discuss with you. Well, you have probably noticed my presence at the Esmeralda the last two nights, and the instant I saw you I at once said to myself, 'Here is the man!'"

Marston bowed without making a reply.

"Matters of state compel me to entrust you with a secret that, from reasons which I will shortly show you, I feel convinced you will find to your benefit to keep locked up in your breast. Briefly, we—that is, the populace—are on the verge of a revolution—a revolution that may burst at any moment—and it was considered advisable that General Guzman, our President, should—anyhow, for the time being—discreetly withdraw. For the matter of that, he leaves the Yellow House to-night; but it is most imperative for the Government party that his absence should not be known to the mob. You follow me?"

Again Marston silently inclined his head.

"Good! Now, in order to effect this purpose, I have called in your assistance."

"Mine?" suddenly ejaculated the bewildered Britisher. "Why—"

"Pardon. One moment. Yes, yours. See." And the officer drew from his pocket a photograph of an elderly man in military uniform, whose breast was resplendent with orders. "This is President Guzman," he continued, handing the portrait to the actor. "You may possibly notice there is a most striking resemblance to yourself, especially when you wear the grey wig I have seen you in. You would merely require the moustache, which I imagine would not prove an insurmountable difficulty, and with a suitable uniform you could easily be mistaken for the original of the portrait."

"Then you want me to—to—" stammered the Britisher.

"To act as the President for twelve hours, Senor Marston."

Rapidly the further details were unfolded, and, after some considerable discussion, ended in the denouement recorded at the beginning of this chapter.

Finding himself helpless to resist, as the men in whose hands he found himself were evidently not to be trifled with, Marston at length, at the general's dictation, wrote a short note to the stage doorkeeper at the Esmeralda, authorising him to hand to the bearer his wig case and "make-up" box; after which, as those whom he could only consider his captors had determined not to lose sight of him, he found himself locked up in a small bed-room, from which there was not any possibility of escape.

A few half-hearted "Vivas!" arose from a crowd of loafers hanging around the gates of the Yellow House on the following afternoon as a closed carriage, in which was seated a grey-headed and grey-moustached individual, in a glittering uniform emerged from its portals; cries to which the occupant of the vehicle responded by raising his hand at a military salute.

It was the hour at which the President usually took the afternoon drive, and many were the curious glances directed towards the turn-out, for already a whisper had gone abroad that President Guzman, fearing what might happen, had fled; and yet there he was, driving along unattended, as usual.

"Ah!" muttered an evil-looking fellow, in a large, slouched hat. "Little he thinks what the end of the drive will be!"

"Hist!" replied his companion. "You thrice fool, speak not so loud. But, come! As we must witness this brave show."

After traversing the broad, open streets, in which the elite of Cabellano delight to disport themselves, the President's carriage turned, and took a course that lay across the large plaza facing the cathedral.

As usual, the space was fairly filled with loungers, and on the steps of the cathedral itself a small group of men were stationed. Suddenly, as the carriage passed them, an arm was raised in the air. A small, spherical object flew towards the vehicle. There was a blinding flash, a terrific roar, mingled with shrieks of women and the stamping of frightened horses, and for the time being the scene was veiled from view by a choking cloud of dust. Although without doubt the missile had been launched at the Presidential carriage, yet, fortunately for its occupant, the aim had been incorrect, for it exploded some distance in the rear. As it was it had the effect of causing the horses to take fright. The coachman was hurled from his box, and the high-spirited animals swerved round, colliding with an iron post. In an instant the vehicle was overturned, when their hoofs soon converted it into fragments, from amongst which a man in a brilliant but torn uniform was trying to extricate himself.

"The President—the President!" shouted the mob, which seemed to have sprung up as if by magic, and they dashed towards the wreckage.

But those nearest suddenly paused in amazement.

Instead of the aged Guzman, there faced them a young man, with clean-shaven face and closely-curling brown hair, for in the struggle to free himself the grey wig and false moustache had been torn off, and Dick Marston, alone and unaided, stood facing an enraged mob.

The hot blood of the Southern American is quickly aroused, and even the few amongst those present, who would have in the ordinary way deplored the means taken to remove the obnoxious President, were filled with rage at the evident trick of which the public had been dupes.

"Treachery! Vengeance!" rose the cries on all sides. "Guzman has gone! Seize the impostor!"

And instantly a mad rush was made; and, fight as he would, Dick Marston was overpowered in a moment, and although the handful of Republican Guards who galloped up made a faint show of going to his assistance, they were either in sympathy with the crowd, or overawed by its numbers.

"To the trees!" arose a shrill cry, that was taken up by hundreds, for by that time the news had spread with lightning rapidity, and the plaza was one seething mass of humanity.

Without uttering a word, but with his teeth clenched tightly, and his clothing torn to ribbons, the Britisher still battled with the savage mob, who bore him shoulder-high, till, reaching a group of tall trees abutting upon the square, a halt was made.

A rope had been procured from somewhere, and with eager hands two villainous-looking ruffians were securing it round his neck, when a third man, forcing his way between them, thrust a thick cloth in the actor's face. Apparently it was soaked in some powerful aesthetic, for he gave one gasp, then fell back upon the shoulders of his would-be executioners, unconscious.

CHAPTER 3.   Plot Against Plot.

WE must now return to Barry Clinton, who, finding his chum had not returned to the chacara the previous night, was prepared to give him some good-natured chaff, and it was not until late in the following morning, when Marston had not put in an appearance at the theatre as usual, that he began to feel really anxious.

"Hallo!" he cried suddenly, as he entered their dressing-room, and noticed the absence of Dick's props. "Here, Sambo you black thief," he called, "come here! What have you been doing with Senor Marston's boxes?"

Obedient to the call, the stage doorkeeper and general factotum entered.

"Me, sar? Why, I gib them to man what call last night. He bring little note from Massa Marston."

"Brought a note! What the devil do you mean?"

"Mean what I say, sar. See here!"

And, diving into his pocket, he drew forth a piece of paper that had not improved in appearance through his keeping.

Clinton snatched it from the negro and held it up to the light. Written on paper headed 15, Calle de la Paz.

"Rummy I wonder what on earth he was up to? That was the address upon the card he had last night."

"I say, Pedro," he shouted, as he caught sight of the musician crossing the stage, "you know everyone in this cussed place. Who is it that lives at 15, Calle de la Paz?"

Thus addressed, the Spaniard turned, and in a few words the Britisher related the story of his friend's invitation, and his own anxiety at his non-appearance.

The man listened quietly, then remained silent for a few seconds, as if revolving the matter in his mind, when, suddenly springing back as if he had received an electric shock, he cried:

"Sante Dios! I see it—I see it! The President—the President!"

"What on earth are you talking about?" demanded Barry Clinton, somewhat angrily.

By way of a reply, Pedro approached the actor, and, drawing him on one side, whispered:

"You understand not. Say nothing, but meet me outside the theatre in five minutes. Your friend's life is in danger—great danger! More I cannot tell you now."

And placing his finger to his lips, he hurried away.

Within the mentioned time the two men once more met at the main entrance to the theatre, and, taking his companion's arm, Pedro hurried forward, nor did he pause till, after traversing several narrow streets, he threw open the door of a third-rate wine-shop.

Once inside, he nodded familiarly to several of the customers, and, seating himself at a small table, called for a bottle of vino tinto, and after it was served he turned to the bewildered actor.

"Senor, we may talk safely here, and I can tell you of what you may not know."

Rapidly he narrated what the reader is already acquainted with, how Dick Marston had been forced to impersonate the President.

"You wonder why I tell you this," he continued. "I knew of the plot all along, because I am in the Secret Service. But one thing I did not know—that Senor Marston was the one to play the part. Two nights ago he saved my life, and now I will try to save his. 'Tis well known to us secret agents that the mob will attempt to assassinate President Guzman as he passes to the cathedral this afternoon. De Llomurcia and his friends care not that" and he snapped his fingers— "for your friend's life, and are only awaiting the attack to pour in the troops that even now are in readiness, as the outrage will give them the opportunity of crushing the revolution with an iron hand. Unless we are careful the senor will be blown to pieces!"

Barry Clinton listened aghast.

"I never heard of such cold-blooded treachery!" at length he stammered out. "You intend to let a man be murdered so that you get an excuse for placing the city under martial law."

"No es nada" (it is nothing), continued Pedro. "What is one life when hundreds will be shot down before this time tomorrow? Ah, here comes the man I want!"—as a seedy-looking individual entered the doors. "Leave not this place till I see you again."

And approaching the newcomer, he led him into an inner room.

For quite half an hour Barry Clinton sat and fidgeted as he continually consulted his watch. All sorts of vague ideas crowded through his brain. First he would go to the police, and claim protection for his friend as a British subject; then he would, at all risks, force his way into the Yellow House, and inform Marston of the danger he was in; and he was just rising from his seat, when Pedro once more seated himself beside him.

"'Tis all arranged, senor," he said quietly.

"What is?"

"Our plan of action to save your friend. But come. We have no time to waste."

And, without vouchsafing any further information, he strode rapidly from the premises.

* * * * *

When we left Dick Marston he had fallen back unconscious upon the shoulders of those who held him, and a howl of execration arose as the man who had thrust the cloth in his face shouted at the top of his voice:

"He is dead! The impostor has died of fright!"

"To the rope! String him up! Riddle him with bullets!"

These, and a hundred other exclamations, could be heard on all sides, for the mob, mad with rage at the deception practised upon them, and unable to wreak their vengeance upon the hated President, were lusting for the blood of the man who had duped them.

"Stay!" cried the stranger, who was evidently well known to many in the crowd. "Why waste good powdery camaradoes, on this British carrion. Viva el populo! We shall want all our bullets before long. Fling him into the canal!"

The idea immediately caught on, and Marston was thrown to the ground as four stalwart men, thrusting all others on one side, seized him and, amidst hoots and yells, bore him in the direction of the water.

They had not, however, proceeded far when a fresh shout arose from the rear of the crowd, and above the cries of the populace, came the crash of musketry; then, before those present could hardly realise what had happened, a squadron of blue-uniformed men, with swords flashing in the sun, were upon them, sabring right and left as their horses ploughed through the living mass. The revolution had broken out, only to be trodden under foot by the iron-shod heel of President Guzman.

* * * * *

It was several days before Dick Marston was sufficiently recovered from the effects of his terrible experiences to understand all that had occurred, and then Barry Clinton enlightened him. How Pedro had placed a couple of men on the steps of the cathedral from where they heard the bomb would be launched, and how at the critical moment they had lurched against the thrower, thus diverting his aim. How it was Pedro himself who had thrust the cloth in his face, rendering him unconscious, and was thus enabled to persuade the mob that he was dead; and how that he—Barry Clinton—aided by Pedro's Secret Service men, had dragged him away from the horses' hoofs when the mad charge of the cavalry was made.

For the rest, the Teatro del Esmeralda was closed for several nights; and as for the revolution, after several hours severe street fighting it was nipped in the bud, and General Guzman held the Presidential reins with an even firmer hand than before.

THE END.

Our MAGAZINE CORNER,
DEVIL'S ISLAND.

Of all the horrors this earth has ever possessed, that of Devil's Island must be listed among the most inhuman and the worst. A mere patch of sand and gravel in the tropic seas, for many, many weary years it was the living grave of thousands of convicts whom France considered unfit for incarceration in her ordinary gaols, and who had, by some miracle of bad fortune, escaped the far more preferable fate of the guillotine.

Bad fortune?—Landru, the Bluebeard of modern France, for one accounted it so. For he reckoned himself lucky that his appeal against the sentence of death having failed, he was at least certain that the terrors of Devil's Island were not for him—as would almost certainly have been the case had his sentence been altered.

Even the prospects of escape were banished from the minds of the majority whose sentence was lifelong, or a shorter term of banishment to that hell on earth which lay twelve miles out at sea. Nevertheless, there have been those in plenty who preferred to risk the dangers of flight, and have essayed the journey of twelve, shark-infested miles of water that cut them off from the mainland of Cayenne in French Guiana, rather than suffer the limit of tortures that can be inflicted out of man's sheer inhumanity to man.

Eighteen hundred convicts a year on an average have made the attempt, pitting their luck against sharks and warders in the first instance, and then, when the pitiless mainland has been reached, against the ravenous wild beasts and poisonous snakes that lurked in the jungles, the burning rays of a brazen sun, or the drenching, numbing rain that falls there almost unceasingly six months in the year; and, by night, the malaria and yellow fever brought creeping over the land by the night-mists from the trackless marshes that form the breeding-place of loathsome, death-dealing animals innumerable.

Of that venturesome eighteen hundred, fifteen hundred were yearly recaptured. The remainder, barring a very occasional complete get-away— and the total for all the years can be counted on the fingers of one hand—died a death whose agonies are unmentionable. Seven hundred of the convicts got their final release each twelvemonth at the hands of the Great Avenger, on the island itself.

And these were the lucky ones. For those who were recaptured were either shot down like dogs or imprisoned in iron cages for the rest of their life, the alternative to caging being the wearing of heavy iron shackles, for as long as breath remained in the poor, tortured body.

It remained for that great Frenchman, Monsieur Herriot, to abolish this settlement where human life was held so cheaply. And it was through the agency of a fearless and outspoken newspaper that this blot was finally removed, but a few months ago, from the escutcheon of that country. So moved was M. Herriot by the newspaper's almost unbelievable account of the shocking atrocities practised on Devil's Island that he ordered a full report to be made officially and sent to him. The result was the closing down of that place of imprisonment which compared unfavourably with the worst of the imagined rigours of Satan's own unholy domain.

At the time of the grim settlement's abolition there were confined there 2,500 convicts, working out a sentence of not less than eight years' hard labour. In most cases they were lifers, on their senses impressed for ever more the fact that of all the great cruelties extant where Mother Nature reigns none could rival in heartlessness and abandoned ferocity that of which man, the over-lord, is capable.

One or two whose names may be reckoned— at least, in France—as household words almost, have for a brief season, left behind them the wicked regime of Devil's Island, only to be sent back there again when the arm of the law stretched out and plucked the fugitive from his hiding-place. There was one whom we will call Henri Apard. He knew the waters around Devil's Island to be teeming with hungry sharks. All the offal of the island—and this included the bodies of convicts who passed to the Great Beyond—was flung to them. So they regularly looked for meals around the island's seaboard.

This man realised that if he attempted to cross on a raft the twelve miles of sea that cut him off from Cayenne, the sharks would surely haul him off before he had gone a dozen yards. So he hit upon the scheme of crawling into the interior of a hollow tree log and trusting to Fate to be carried to the mainland shore.

Thus he was found by an American vessel, miles out at sea. The captain of the vessel took pity on him. He took him aboard, gave him a little money, and put him ashore at a point where he could make good his escape. Unable to resist the homing instinct, the fugitive returned to his native France, where his recapture was effected—and the island claimed its own again.